THE LIGHT

A NOVEL

By

Robert Hammond

NewWay Press

Published in the United States
by New Way Press.
www.newwaypress.com

Library of Congress Control Number: 2013906756

ISBN-13:978-0615796567
ISBN-10: 0615796567

DEDICATION

✳

This book is dedicated to the
Light within you and all around you.

ACKNOWLEDGEMENTS

✳

Thanks to all of the people who helped make this book a reality, especially Abel Adams who allowed me to tell his story. Thanks also to the many people who assisted along the way as The Light appeared in previous incarnations. Special thanks to Ron Vervick, Executive Director of Whiteside Manor, Mike Soccio, Riverside County Chief Deputy District Attorney, and Governor Jerry Brown for your assistance, guidance, and pardon. Utmost thanks to my wife Lesa for her enduring love and patience, as well as to my mother, father, and son who believed in me and supported me through all the years in spite of myself.

The first step to peace is to stand still in the Light.
~ George Fox

PROLOGUE

✴

By the time you read this I'll be gone.

I woke up blindfolded and tied to a chair. A distant voice whispered, "Have you seen the light?" I shook and struggled desperately to loosen myself from my bonds.

A California earthquake rattled my apartment and I woke up from the dream to see books falling from the shelf. Once again, I had fallen asleep at my desk while working on my latest manuscript. Scattered stacks of yellow legal tablets surrounded me. I rubbed my eyes and looked around the room. I turned and saw the framed Picasso drawing of *The Unknown Masterpiece* hanging on my wall at a crooked angle.

BANG! BANG! BANG! The sound of somebody pounding at the door. I mumbled, "Who is it?"

"Are you awake?" Grace Hanuman entered the unlocked door of my apartment and looked around the disheveled living room. She picked up a book that had fallen from the bookcase and whispered the title, "Parsifal." She gazed at me with intense curiosity as I straightened the *Unknown Masterpiece* on the wall. "Do you remember that Abel's sentencing hearing is today? It starts in less than an hour. You are coming aren't you?"

"Ready when you are," I said, still rubbing the sleep from my eyes.

"I'll see you there." Grace headed out the door.

***

BANG! BANG! BANG! Abel Adams snapped back into reality as the judge's gavel slammed against the bench. "I hereby sentence you to eighteen months in the county jail." As I sat in the back of the courtroom with Grace, I watched in disappointment as the bailiff handcuffed our childhood friend and dragged him off to his fate.

Little did I know that everything was about to change in ways that I could not have possibly imagined. Eventually, Abel would ask me to help write this book, revealing the story of his life, a spiritual journey so profound and surprising that it is almost impossible to comprehend. You may not believe what happened as I can scarcely believe some of it myself. But, like gravity, some things are true whether we believe them or not.

CHAPTER 1

BIRTH TRAUMA

✳

Have you seen the light?

Cast from my Eden,
Like when I was first born.
Naked and ashamed.
Afraid to be touched
Or even to be seen
By anyone.

Just let me go back deep inside
My solitary womb
Where I was safe.
It's not my time yet.
I'm not ready to come out.
Please don't make me come outside.
Just let me stay here
In the darkness of my safe cocoon.

If this is life
Then I don't want to be here.
Keep your cold, metallic tables,
Your antiseptics,
And your blinding lights.
For I don't want to see or feel anything.
It hurts too much
And only Demerol
Can ease the pain

Have you seen the light?

Who is Abel Adams? He closed his eyes so nobody could see him.

Wednesday's child. Double Pisces. Scorpio rising on a February midnight beneath an auspicious new moon. Abel's father, an Army Lieutenant, parachuted from a C-119 flying boxcar into the black sky over Southeast Asia on a dark mission with the 82nd Airborne Division.

His mother screamed in agony and loneliness.

An eternity of darkness gave way as contractions jolted Abel from his place of peace and safety. He pondered the fundamental question, *Who am I?*

I AM THAT, his rhythmic mantra reminded him, conscious of all that was around him since the moment of his conception and before the beginning. Then sudden pain. The umbilical cord wrapped itself around his neck like a hangman's noose. He was drowning in an amniotic sea of primordial pain.

2

Where once two heartbeats pounded as one, now separate rhythms sounded. The delicate balance had begun to break. Poured out like water, all his bones were out of joint. *My God, my God. Why have you forsaken me?*

The Three Assassins, Fear, Guilt, and Resentment, stalked and surrounded him. Like roaring lions tearing their prey, they opened their mouths wide against him.

Then sparkled the warm tingling sensation as the sweet taste of Demerol dissolved the pain. Abel melted into a sea of bliss as he surrendered to its seduction, and everything turned into magic and light.

The slap across his buttocks awakened him again to the pain of his new life.

He gasped for breath and cried. Who am I?

Loneliness embraced him as he opened his eyes and stared at the bright white ceiling.

His groans became thoughts forming from the void like new galaxies, spinning forth as the light of ten thousand stars.

***

When Abel was two years old, his Aunt Delilah gave him the juice of brandied cherries before Thanksgiving dinner and he became so alive and outspoken during that his performance spellbound everyone at the table. She prophesied, "This boy's going to be a preacher one day."

Abel's father taught him how to pray: "Now I lay me down to sleep. I pray the Lord my soul to keep. If I should die before I wake, I pray the Lord my soul to take." Abel pondered the implications. *If I should die before I wake? My soul to take? My soul to take?*

Abel's family lived in a predominately-black neighborhood in Norville, Maryland. He attended an all-black nursery school while his father pursued his doctorate in Applied Physics at Banneker University, a private college catering to the black bourgeoisie. In one of Abel's first memories of him, his father lay slumped across a heap of textbooks, exhausted. His mother worked as a secretary while his father finished his degree.

Abel started stealing. He stole his dad's pearl-handled penknife from the top of the dresser. He thought it would be fun to play with and show the other kids. His nursery school teacher discovered the knife in his pocket after he peed in his pants during naptime and had to change his clothes in the back of the classroom. His mother had to leave work early to come and take him home. "If you ever do something like this again I will slap you into another world. Understand?"

He nodded and wondered whether she was referring to the knife or the pants peeing.

Later that evening, Abel heard the ice cream truck outside their apartment. He ran into the living room pleading, "Can I have some money for the ice cream man? He's out there in the street right now!"

His mother wrinkled her brow and said, "No. We're getting ready to have dinner and I don't want you to ruin your appetite."

"But Mommy, all the other kids are going to get some."

His father hopped into the fray, "Didn't you hear your mother? She said no."

Dejected, Abel went into his room to pout for a while, when he suddenly remembered seeing some money on his parents' dresser. He peeked around the corner and then dashed into their room, snatching a bill that was lying next to his father's cufflinks and headed back for the front door.

"Dinner will be in twenty minutes," his mother called to him as he headed out the door.

"Okay," he replied, slamming the door behind him.

Abel returned a few minutes later, his arms laden with ice cream treats for their desert. His father looked up, wide-eyed and said, "What the… there must be twenty dollars worth of ice cream there!"

His mother turned and saw his purchases. She glared at him and put her hands on her hips. "Give me those and go to your room."

***

In the summer of 1963, Abel's family moved to Eden Valley, a sleepy little town along the northern California coast. The temperature was mild and the land was green with agriculture. The migrant farm workers came to plant and pick strawberries, grapes, lettuce, broccoli, spinach, and artichokes. Just thirty miles to the south was the small community of Los Tecatos – heroin capital of northern California.

Abel's father was hired as a physics professor at Eden University. The chancellor wanted to bring more "color" into the school. The board of regents agreed that having a black professor would set the school apart and make the campus livelier, so they gave Abel's father a new Cadillac and paid him a handsome salary.

On Abel's first day of school, he stood at the bus stop in front of his house. The bus pulled up and he stepped aboard holding his Leave it to Beaver lunch pail close to his side. He smiled nervously at the other children. A blonde haired boy pointed at him and said, "Look at Blackie!" The other kids laughed and pointed.

Another kid patted Abel on the head and said, "Hey Blackie!" Abel grabbed the boy's hand and twisted it behind his back, causing the boy to groan in agony.

The bus driver stood up and turned toward Abel. "You get up here right now and sit down, you little trouble maker." Abel let the boy out of the arm lock and walked to the front of the bus. The driver pointed to the floor next to him and said, "Now sit there and keep your mouth shut."

When Abel got to school, his teacher called him up to the front of the class and said, "As one of the only colored boys here you're going to have to set an example for your race."

Abel's family lived on the predominantly white west side where they attended a predominantly white church and Robert was only other black kid in Abel's elementary school. Robert sat in the back of the class, unnoticed.

Once, when Abel was drawing a house with a black crayon, the teacher told him, "Black is a horrid color." Abel hung his head. The teacher proceeded to read the story of Little Black Sambo to the class. He hid his face in his arms against the desktop, eyes closed, invisible. He dug his nails into the flesh of his forearms while the class stared at him.

Abel's brother, Jesse, was born in 1962 and Abel was no longer the center of attention.

Some neighbor boys invited Abel to go exploring in the woods across the street from where they lived. They led him down a dark wooded path and then they started running. When he tried to chase after them, he ran into a swarm of yellow jackets. He could hear them laughing as he ran home screaming.

If only I could be someone else, he thought. Someone white.

Abel's family went to see West Side Story at the drive-in. Fantasy and reality melted into one, as Abel became Tony, the white lead character. He was in love with Maria, the Puerto Rican girl whom he could never have, trapped in a cycle of self-destruction and mixed-loyalties. He choked back the tears at the ending when they sang, "There's a Place for Us."

He found his identity in that larger-than-life character on the screen, the leader of the Jets. The next day, the school playground became the stage for his fantasies, as Abel zigzagged across the blacktop, chasing the other kids with an invisible switchblade.

The bell rang and the kids lined up to return to class, laughing about the dramatic lunch hour, patting Abel on the back for his amazing performance. As he stood in line, snapping his fingers and singing "The Jet Song," a teacher grabbed him and said, "You're coming with me."

"What did I do?" he asked, holding his arms out to his sides in feigned innocence.

The teacher pointed to the principal's office. "Shut up and come with me."

Abel sat in the office for an hour before the principal came into the room. She told him, "We've talked with your mother and she gave us permission to proceed with discipline for your behavior on the playground today."

"We were just having fun like in the movie," he replied.

The principal stood up behind his desk and walked around the front where he towered over him. "Stand up and slide that chair over here."

Abel just sat there with his arms folded and shook his head.

The principal grabbed him by the arms and lifted him to his feet. "Bend over and hold onto the back of the chair."

SWAT! The paddle landed squarely against his backside. He fought to hold back the tears, more of broken pride and spirit than of physical pain. Yet that was real too.

Who am I? Nobody. Nothing. Nonexistent. He closed his eyes so nobody could see him

***

The next day Abel sat in his third grade classroom; he closed his eyes and pictured himself standing before the throng. *"Ladies and gentlemen, I present to you the President of the United States, Abel Adams."* The applause was deafening.

Then he woke up.

"The President has just been shot," the principal announced over the intercom just before lunch. A hush fell over the classroom. The teacher gasped. A couple of kids started to cry. The principal continued, "Boys and girls, I know this is difficult to understand, but I want you to all remain calm." The bell rang for lunch.

Abel's house was just a few blocks away from the school and he ran home as fast as he could. He always walked home for lunch and his mom was just putting some cream of mushroom soup and a peanut butter and jelly sandwich on the table when he arrived. "Abel. You're just in time for lunch," she said.

He glanced at the television, which was off. He stood there quietly, and then looked at her. "Mom, they shot the President."

She shook her head and laughed. "You shouldn't say things like that."

"Mom, I mean it. They just told us at school. The President was shot." He went to the television and turned it on. Walter Cronkite was narrating the tragic event.

His mother ran into the living room and watched the black and white screen in horror. "Oh my dear God...no!" Then she crumbled to the floor and lay there sobbing while Jessie ran to her and wailed. Abel stood there silently for a moment, then knelt to the floor and put his arms around his mother and his brother. "Don't cry. Don't cry. Please, don't cry," he whispered.

***

Abel soon developed a fascination with science fiction and fantasy novels. His favorite story was *A Wrinkle in Time*, by Madeleine L'Engle, about a strange child who escaped the pain of reality through a time warp known as the tesseract. He longed desperately for a way to escape his present reality and travel into another place in time.

"I know what I want to do when I grow up," he proudly boasted to his father.

His father seemed mildly annoyed by the interruption of his evening purveyance of the latest issue of Scientific American. "I thought you said you were going to be a nuclear physicist." He flipped the page nonchalantly.

"No. That was last week."

"So what's it going to be this week, oceanographer?" he asked without glancing up from his magazine.

"I'm going to be a writer!"

"Writers starve to death."

Abel turned on his heel and ran to his room, slamming the door behind him.

***

Abel was eight years old when he was baptized at Eden Valley Community Church.

"Do you believe that Jesus Christ was the only begotten Son of God, who died for your sins, was buried and rose again on the third day?" The Reverend's voice echoed against the tile baptistery. The water was cold.

"Yes," he replied meekly.

"I baptize you in the name of the Father, the Son, and the Holy Spirit." The Reverend's voice disappeared as Abel sank beneath a sea of pain. The water entered his nostrils and he gagged.

He flashed back to his birth. Drowning in amniotic fluid. Umbilical chord wrapped around his neck like a hangman's noose. He choked. Coughed. Gasped for air.

Murderous rage. Hatred of God and angels sank beneath a sea of sorrow. Washed in the water of life.

Surrendered to the eternal. Dead and buried with Christ.

Yes, he did believe, but...

So many questions yet unanswered. So many deeds undone. At age eight his heart had only just begun to lust for the Tree of Knowledge. Duality. Good and evil. An unfulfilled yearning pounded deep within him. His sins had been forgiven and he had only just begun to sin.

He emerged from the water of life, coughing and spitting.

"Amazing grace, how sweet the sound..." the choir harmonized.

Later that day, Abel chased his little brother Jesse through the house and pounded on his back with his fist as he ran for cover. Abel had caught Jesse playing with his toys without asking him. His rage exploded.

"Abel!" his mom yelled. "Go to your room and stay there until you learn to calm down and behave yourself."

"But it was his fault! He went through my stuff."

She put her hands on her hips. "You just came from church, for goodness' sake. Didn't you learn anything?"

"I guess not," he shrugged.

She frowned and took a deep breath. "Go to your room."

He slammed the door as loneliness embraced him with a chokehold. He picked up his Bible from the top of the dresser and threw it against the door. "I hate you! I hate you! I hate you! You're all against me."

As his sobbing subsided, he sank into sleep. He dreamt that he was a butterfly, desperately seeking, desperately dreaming.

CHAPTER 2

TURN ON, TUNE IN, DROP OUT

✳

Desperately running
Desperately seeking
Desperately dreaming
Chasing the elusive dance
Of a butterfly
As it flutters
Just beyond my grasp
In the sunlight
As it glistens
In my desperate tears

I continue...
Desperately running
Desperately seeking
Desperately dreaming
Till I awaken

To the blinding light
 Of reality
To discover that
I am the butterfly
Being chased
As it flutters
Just beyond the grasp

Of the ONE
Desperately running
Desperately seeking
Desperately dreaming
Desperately running
Desperately seeking
Desperately dreaming

Abel stood alone in the middle of the family room, petrified by what the man on television was saying. His name was Timothy Leary. "Turn on. Tune in. Drop out," he intoned. His sinister smile reminded Abel of the Twilight Zone episode where the devil took a murdered gangster on a tour of Hell and the gangster thought he was in Heaven.

Abel was terrified of his proposal. "Insanity," he whispered. He imagined them taking over the world, drug crazed fiends with sinister smiles. No way. Never. Not me.

Max Scofield was Abel's next-door neighbor – an aspiring musician. He sang and played the guitar and taught Abel all about the history of jazz, blues, and rock and roll. Max was also well versed in popular culture and taught Abel all about the California scene.

Once, on a nature hike, they came across some yellow wildflowers. Abel picked one. "What are these?"

"Poppies," Max replied with a cautious tone. "Don't touch them. They'll make you go crazy."

He let the California poppy fall from his hand as the words, They'll make you go crazy, echoed in his mind. He dusted the pollen from his hands and continued up the trail.

In the summer of 1969, the family went on vacation to Babylonia, a bustling port city about fifty miles north of Eden Valley. Abel felt swept away by the excitement of the love generation and came home with love beads, a headband, and a peace sign. He bought a set of Yarrow Sticks along with a copy of *The I Ching*, or *Book of Changes*, a fortune-telling system used by the ancient Chinese.

Abel also purchased a black 8-ball which, when asked a question and turned upside down, would provide such answers as "not a good idea," "try again," "could be," or "yes, definitely."

While the family was shopping, somebody stole the luggage from their rooftop compartment. "Probably some lost soul," his father responded. Abel wondered what he meant by "lost soul."

Abel returned from Babylonia with a renewed attitude. Something mystical had happened, and he knew that life would never be the same for him. The *I Ching* confirmed that his destiny was about to change.

Abel became fascinated with the mystical. He joined an occult book-of-the-month club and began reading such classics as *Yoga, Youth and Reincarnation* by Jess Stearn and *Autobiography of a Yogi* by Paramahansa Yogananda. He knew that human potential was unlimited, and felt determined to expand his consciousness to the highest degree possible.

Abel and Jesse played a game called *Kreskin's ESP*, based on the parapsychology experiments at Duke University. The game consisted of a set of cards containing one of four patterns: a circle, a triangle, a plus sign, and a star. The object was to develop one's extrasensory perception powers by guessing which card the other person was holding. The game also included a pendulum, which they would hold in one hand while asking various questions. If the pendulum swung up and down that would mean yes. If it swung from left to right that would be a no. When that got boring, Abel and Jesse got out the Ouija Board. One day Abel asked who was controlling the board. They held the pointer lightly with their fingertips as it skirted across the board spelling out the letters S-A-T-A. Before it could finish spelling out the word, they both screamed and ran out of the room.

By the time Abel entered high school, he started hanging out with a new crowd. Yogi Santana had slicked back black hair and long sideburns. The first time Yogi came over after school, Abel's mother shot him a dirty look, and after he left she shook her head slowly and said, "I don't like that boy."

He sighed. "But you don't even know him."

"He just looks like bad news," she said.

Abel turned away and slipped into his room, slamming the door and turning on Led Zeppelin at full blast.

The next day, Abel walked to the little shack in the back of Yogi's mother's house after school.

"You ready to try this out?" Yogi asked.

"Yeah," he replied, raising his eyebrow twice.

"Okay. Take in about ten long breaths and then hold it, and then I'll give you a bear hug."

Abel did as Yogi said, and the effect was an electric rush of tingling sensations from head to toe. This is it. *Electric Avenue. Zap City.* Then he lapsed into unconsciousness. He was out for about five seconds but it seemed like a lot longer.

"Wicked!" Abel exclaimed as he got up from the floor. "That was cool. Let's do it again."

Yogi laughed uncontrollably and gave Abel a shove. "My turn." He took ten deep breaths and motioned for Abel to grab him around the chest. He did and Yogi got this crazy look on his face as he slid to the floor.

Yogi got up and pulled out a pack of Marlboros, tapping the pack against the palm of his hand. He put a cigarette in his mouth and lit it, taking a big pull while letting it hang from his lips. He allowed the smoke to drift out the side of his mouth as he pointed the pack Abel's way and said, "Want one?"

"Yeah, man." Abel grabbed for the pack and tapped it against his palm, knocking half of the cigarettes onto the floor. Yogi looked down at him, shaking his head.

Abel picked the smokes up and stuck all but one of them back into the pack. He let it hang out of the side of his mouth and grabbed a book of matches from the table. He fired up and coughed, sending the cigarette flying across the room where it landed on a stack of old newspapers. He ran over and grabbed the burning cigarette just as the newspapers started to smolder. He held it between his thumb and forefinger and brought it back to his lips as he stomped on the newspapers to keep them from blazing. He took a drag and blew it out quickly as his eyes watered and a fought the urge to gag.

Yogi blew smoke rings. "Thirsty?"

Abel coughed. "Yeah. Watcha got?"

Yogi got up from the couch. "Come on." He motioned his head toward the door. Abel got up and followed him out the door.

They walked down to the corner grocery store. Before they went inside, Abel pulled his empty pockets inside out and said, "I don't have any bread, man."

Yogi smiled. "Don't worry about it. Just follow my lead." They walked into the store and went to the back where the cooler was. A young mother with her baby in a stroller was at the counter buying a six-pack of beer. He watched Yogi as he slipped a bottle of Boone's Farm under his coat. Yogi nodded his head toward the cooler and whispered, "Go ahead."

His heart began pounding and he felt sick to his stomach. His palms were cold and sweaty, and he looked over his shoulder to see that the clerk was looking the other way. He reached in, grabbed a bottle of Strawberry Hill, and slid it beneath his coat. He held it in place with one arm as he stuck his other hand in his pocket and tried to look cool. Yogi and Abel strolled by the clerk. Abel avoided eye contact as they stepped into the afternoon chill. As soon as they got to the corner they took off running all the way back to Yogi's house, where they collapsed on the couch and busted up laughing until their eyes ran with tears and their stomachs hurt.

The cheap wine went down cool and sweet, and Abel could feel warmth in the pit of his stomach. Yogi took a big gulp and belched. He lit up a smoke and Abel did the same. It tasted better this time as he blew the smoke out slowly.

Suddenly, Abel looked at his watch and realized his parents had told him to be home by five o'clock that day so they could go and have their family portrait taken at the church. He jumped up and headed toward the door. "Hey, I just remembered something I gotta do. See ya later, man."

Yogi took another swig and said, "What's the big hurry? We're just getting buzzed."

Abel put the cigarette out in an ashtray and looked at his watch again. He shook his head. "Sorry, man. I really gotta go. Check ya later, dude." He headed out the door and ran all the way home.

He arrived through the front door just in time to change.

"Where have you been?" his mother demanded, her hands on her hips.

He shrugged. "I just stopped by a friend's house."

"Hurry up and change. We're going to be late." She pointed toward his room.

"Okay! Okay!" He clamped his hands over his ears.

Everybody was waiting in the car when he came out of the house, having changed into a yellow short-sleeve shirt and blue slacks. When he got into the car, Jessie said, "It smells like something's burning." Abel shot him an angry glance and put his finger to his lips in a "shut up" motion.

As the photographer snapped the picture, Abel was still reeling from the effects of the wine and tobacco.

The next day at school, he ran into Yogi outside of his first period class. "Hey, how's it going?" Abel said, as he slapped Yogi on the back.

"Lousy, man. My mom grounded me for not coming home last night, my girlfriend dumped me, and I'm flunking every class except for shop." Yogi sat down on the brick wall along the main walkway and hung his head. "I think I'll just become a junkie. Then I'll only have one problem to worry about."

Abel looked at Yogi for a moment and realized he was deadly serious. He looked away and thought, *But what a problem.*

He didn't see Yogi at school the next day or the day after that. A couple of days later, Abel read an article in the Eden Valley Times about a group of boys who had gotten caught sniffing spray paint. One of them, Yogi Santana, almost died in the hospital. Abel went to visit him in the hospital, but he had already left against medical advice.

A few days later Abel and Yogi were walking down North Main Street when they stopped in front of a new sign above a little storefront. It read, "Hai Karate School of Martial Arts."

Abel jumped into a karate stance, holding his hands out flat in front of him. Yogi danced around like a prizefighter, shuffling back and forth on his feet, rubbing his thumb against the side of his nose.

"I'm Bruce Lee," Abel said as he executed a spinning back kick, stopping just inches in front of Yogi's face.

"I'm Ali!" Yogi shuffled back a foot or so, then backed up against the wall, bouncing back with a flurry of fast punches, dazzling Abel for a moment, as Abel danced around Yogi's side and came up behind him with a light tap to the back of the head with the back of his hand. "Gotcha, man. That would have knocked you out!"

Yogi leaned up against the building, catching his breath, his forehead laced with sweat. "Aw, man, that wasn't nothing, boy. I would have come back with rope a dope."

Abel laughed. "The only dope here is you."

They peeked inside the building, watching a row of young kids marching up and down on the mats, blocking and punching in rhythm as the elderly Asian man barked out foreign sounding commands. Abel said, "I love karate man. I want to sign up."

"Not me, man," Yogi said, shaking his head. "I'll stick to good old USA boxing. None of that weird, Oriental stuff for this kid."

Abel enrolled the next day and within a few months, the sensei promoted him to purple belt, and he entered a tournament at the Canaan Beach convention center. He lost badly in the first three rounds and his opponent swiftly eliminated him from the competition. A hard sidekick to the kidney knocked him to his knees and left him gasping, almost landing him in the hospital. He returned home pissing blood.

He continued his lessons for a few more months, but as he started involving himself more and more in his new crowd of friends, his interests in other things subsided. He grew his hair into a long afro and wrapped it in a headband like Jimi Hendrix. He wore bell-bottom jeans, a fringed jacket, and wire-rimmed glasses.

Jay Hanuman was a tall, skinny, mixed-race kid with a blonde afro. His father was white and his mother was black. Jay was about a year older than Abel was and was a brown belt in his karate class. They dropped acid together a few times during class and tripped out on the trails of light that flowed from their hands and feet while they did their katas.

Jay invited Abel to his class on African American History. Jay was the lightest skinned kid in the class and people often thought he was white. Abel felt a little strange being in a room with so many black people because he was usually the only black kid in a class full of white people. He stayed though, because he knew that black history was a cool thing to know about.

One other face stood out in the class: a thin Hispanic girl with dark eyes that glistened enticingly. She turned around from the seat in front of him, smiled broadly, and said, "Hi, I'm Cindy. Are you new?"

He smiled back. "No. I'm just hanging out today with my friend Jay. I didn't feel like going to P.E. class."

Cindy Summers was two years older than Abel was. She captured his heart immediately. She wore her long, straight brown hair parted in the middle, and she had rose-colored glasses.

After class Jay said, "Hey why don't we all go over to my house and smoke some pot."

Cindy said, "Far out."

The three of them were walking down a back alley when Jay pulled out a joint. He fired it up and took a hit, then passed it on to Cindy who smiled at Abel, totally ignoring Jay. She took a delicate puff and giggled while she tried to hold in the smoke. She handed the joint to Abel and their hands touched knowingly. He took a big hit and passed it back to Jay, who was trying to act as if he didn't care about the sparks between Cindy and Abel.

Jay took a hit and said, "Man this is some good weed. I can get all you want. I've got connections."

Cindy and Abel stopped, gazed into each other's eyes with longing, and their lips touched. They kissed for an eternity and their hearts merged, melting into a sea of bliss.

Jay kept on walking and said over his shoulder, "Hey if you guys want to get some more of this good weed, you better come on." He kept walking as Abel and Cindy kept standing there kissing.

"Cindy tomorrow is Saturday and my parents won't be home. Why don't you come over and we can hang out?" Abel held both of her hands in his.

"I'd love to."

They parted ways and Abel walked home on a cloud of infatuation.

The next morning his family packed up for a day at the beach. His mom knocked on his bedroom door.

"Abel, are you sure you don't want to come? It will be fun."

"No. That's okay. I'm not feeling well. I'd rather stay home." As soon as everybody left, he jumped out of bed and started cleaning his room like crazy. He jumped in the shower and started singing, "Sunshine of Your Love," by the Cream. He dried off, dressed, picked out his afro, and sprayed it with Natural-Sheen so it was all curly and cool-looking, like Jimi Hendrix. Then he lit up some incense and put the finishing touches on his room. He put on a Crosby, Stills, Nash & Young album so it would be playing "Woodstock" just as Cindy came to the door. He turned up the volume. She said she would be there around noon. It was 12:05. Then it was 12:35 and he put the needle back at the beginning of the album to start it over again. Then it was 1:05. Then 3:05 and he was listening to "4 + 20" over and over again... *"Why am I so alone? Where is my woman? Can I bring her home?"*

Cindy never showed up.

He saw her at school on Monday morning walking next to a frizzy-haired freak with John Lennon glasses. He asked, "What happened? I thought you were going to come over on Saturday?"

"I was going to come but Eddie here...," she nodded toward the freak standing next to her, "invited me to Free Beach and we were having so much fun that we didn't want to leave. I hope you're not mad." Free Beach was a hidden stretch of beach near Gull where hippies frolicked naked in the sun as they drank wine, smoked pot, and made love in the sand. How could Abel possibly be upset about Cindy going to a nude beach with Eddie?

He shook his head and smiled to hide his pain. "No big deal." He turned and walked away before the tears began to trace hot paths down his cheeks.

Abel headed over to Yogi Santana's place. Yogi was sitting on the couch sniffing gold spray paint. He handed Abel a paint soaked rag in a plastic bag. Abel started huffing and the sparks in his head began to ignite like fireworks. He sat in a stupor, staring at nothing in particular and a smile crossed his lips. *I am a doper. At last, I've found a place where I belong. Being a doper is easy. You just have to make getting high your main priority, and I don't have a problem doing that. The more dope I do, the higher my status. The more different I am, the more I'm the same. It doesn't matter that I'm only 14, that I'm black, that my family is wealthy, or that I'm Christian. I can just do my own thing and stay stoned. I finally fit in. I'm home.*

Yogi looked up from his paint bag for a moment and said, "Chicks suck, huh?"

Abel looked over at him and said, "Yeah, they sure do. And that sucks."

CHAPTER 3

HIGH SCHOOL DAZE

✴

The school bus made stops on both sides of town before dropping off at Eden Valley High. The black girls stared at Abel and giggled.

"He a rich kid," he overhead one say.

"He sure is fine," another whispered.

"Well, he gonna be mine," said still another girl, who stood up and turned toward Abel.

She sure is bold, Abel thought.

The girl walked back and sat down beside him, smiling coyly. His cheeks heated with embarrassment. He thought, *She smells of cheap perfume and sweat. I'm afraid of her power.*

She scooted closer to him. "You cute," she said. "What's your name?" She smiled seductively.

He felt a surge of hormones react within a place deep within him and took a deep, slow breath; beads of sweat began to form on his forehead. "Abel," he mumbled, hardly glancing in her direction. He saw the other girls whispering and laughing in the background. He opened his math book and began flipping through the pages, then looked out the window, avoiding her gaze.

"My name's Keisha." She pointed to his math book. "You taking Algebra?"

"Yeah." Abel opened the book and pretended to read.

"Dang, I flunked Basic."

He sighed. He knew that he could never relate to a girl like this. Keisha was the first black girl he knew who wasn't a relative. He felt strangely uncomfortable revisiting the race from which he had been for so long estranged, alienated by the distance of economics and a few city blocks. Abel's family lived within the upper class white neighborhood for so long that they felt they truly belonged there.

The ritual continued over the next couple of days and he began to relax in her presence. One day she said, "Do you know about the Sadie Hawkins?"

"The what?"

"The Sadie Hawkins. It's a dance where the girls invite the boys and everybody gets all dressed up and has a real good time."

"I'm not all that into stuff like that." He looked out the window as the bus rumbled down Broadway.

Keisha said, "You like to get high?"

He looked at her and smiled. "Maybe." They both laughed as the bus came to her stop. He got off with her.

"Come on in. My brother's here with his friends and they got all kind of beer and weed."

After Abel's third can of beer he was already drunk, and he followed Keisha into a dark garage where he lost his last shred of innocence.

***

The Fourth of July Abel hitchhiked to Reston Beach with Yogi. Yogi had taught him things like how to surf and how to roll a good joint. When they arrived in Reston, they smoked a couple joints of Acapulco Gold and headed into a place called Rick's. The jukebox was playing *"Psychedelic Shack."* They looked at each other with half-closed eyes and laughed.

Yep, we're in the right place, he thought. The place had pool tables and pinball machines.

Yogi pointed to a table in the back and said, "Let's sit over there so we can check out the hot chicks."

The waitress came up to them and asked, "What'll you guys have?" She had dark eyes and wore red hot pants.

"I'll have a Coke," Yogi said.

"Yeah, me too," Abel said. "And some fries, too."

A girl with hair of auburn waves like an angel sat alone. Her green eyes gazed back at Abel's with longing. Her magnetism pulled him into her aura. She shook her hips to the music as she approached then held out her hand and motioned with her finger for him to come to her. He stood up and took her hand as they spun onto the dance floor. He held her close and she whispered, "I'm Jasmine."

"You smell good."

"Patchouli oil."

"Yum." He kissed her on the lips and she pressed her body hard against his.

She whispered, "Let's go see the sunset and watch the fireworks."

Abel waved at Yogi, who lifted his Coke in his direction in a toast as Abel and Jasmine turned and slipped outside and ran toward the beach.

She led him to the far end of the beach, away from the crowds. She pulled him to the ground. "Take off all your clothes," she whispered as she rubbed her hand against his thigh. He complied without hesitation. Destiny unfolded and she gave her virgin body to him behind hidden dunes of sand as the sun kissed the sea.

The music of the Isley Brothers serenaded them from a distance. Then the fireworks exploded overhead in a spectacular display as their frenzied passions exploded into oneness, leaving them breathless.

The red sun rose above the dunes as dawn awakened them. Abel felt naked and ashamed. He didn't want to look at her anymore. She still felt like gazing. She kissed him on the lips and wrapped her arms around him tight. Too tight. He pulled back and looked around to see if anybody was watching as he pulled up his pants and started to get up. She reached out and tried to pull him back down.

"I gotta go," he said as he started to walk away. He could hear her weeping as he continued walking away without looking back.

Yogi was sitting in a beach chair, smoking a cigarette, next to a couple of girls in bikinis. He looked and smiled as he saw Abel approach. "Where ya been, bro?"

"Just out having fun." Abel took a seat in the sand.

Yogi put out his cigarette in the sand. "Let's blow this dump."

They headed toward the highway onramp and passed a joint back and forth. "So what happened with your girlfriend?" Yogi asked as he passed the joint Abel's way.

Abel took a long drag and let it out slowly. "She was cool." He lifted the joint in a toast, "Wine, weed, and women!"

Yogi took the joint, lifted it in a salute and smiled. "Wine, weed, and women. What more is there?" A pickup truck pulled up and a longhaired guy smiled and pointed toward the back. They hopped in and rode the highway back down to Eden Valley.

They jumped out and thanked the driver as he nodded his head and pulled off. They started walking into town and Yogi said, "Reston Beach was cool, but we ought to see how the real hippies live."

"Real hippies?"

"Yeah, you know, the ones in the big cities, like Babylonia and Angel City"

"You mean like just take off and go?"

"Why not?" Yogi kicked a rock and shrugged his shoulders.

"What about our parents?"

"Well, I don't know about you, but I hate my step-dad and he hates me. My real dad is in Texas. One of these days I'm going to go see him."

"You talking about just running away from home?"

"Sure, it'll be far out, man."

"I know that Jay Hanuman ran away a couple of times. I remember him saying something about staying away from crazy freaks in Babylonia."

"OK, then. We head south. This time we'll go in style."

He followed Yogi to his house and opened up the garage door. Before them, in gleaming red and white glory, was his step-dad's Honda 50. Yogi put his fingers to his lips. "SHHHH." Slowly he wheeled the bike out of the driveway as Abel stood there wondering what to do. Yogi pulled down the garage door and got on the bike. The key was still in the ignition. "Get on."

Abel hopped on the back and they headed back down the highway. It was getting dark when they turned onto Logan Pass, a shortcut through the hills. They drove by a place that looked like a motel, with a row of bungalows on one side and a restaurant on the other side of the driveway. "Let's check it out," Yogi said as they pulled up and parked the bike around the side of the building behind some trees. There was a long porch in front with a couple of big wooden benches.

"I'm worn out," Abel said as he stretched out on one of the benches and closed his eyes. Yogi sprawled out on the other bench and fell asleep without saying a word.

Suddenly a man standing over them with a big flashlight awakened them. "Hey, what's going on here?"

Yogi answered, "Hey, man, we're just trying to crash out for the night. We don't have any money and no place to stay."

The man held his flat hand at an angle in front of him as if he was going to make a karate chop. "Well, I'm the innkeeper here and I'll kick your asses if you don't get away from around here."

"Sorry, man," Abel said as he sat up and wiped his eyes. "Don't worry, man, we're leaving." Yogi and Abel stood to their feet and started to walk away.

"Hey, not so fast you two. You look a little young to be here in the middle of the night. Do your parents know where you are?"

"Yeah they know we're out late, but they don't care," Yogi said.

"I ought to call the cops," the innkeeper said. "I think you guys are runaways."

"No, honest, man." Yogi held up three fingers in scout's honor.

The man stared at them for a few seconds, looked up, and then nodded his head. "Wait here." He turned and walked toward the office.

Yogi turned to Abel. "Let's get out of here. I think this fool's gonna call the cops."

Abel lifted up his hand and said, "No, wait. Let's just wait a minute." Yogi shrugged his shoulders and sighed. Moments later the innkeeper returned with a set of keys and opened up a room with a pair of twin beds.

"This room is vacant. I'm going to let you boys stay here tonight, but you gotta leave first thing in the morning."

"Thanks, man," Abel said. Yogi and Abel looked at each other, looked back at him, and then entered the room, closing the door behind them. They jumped onto the beds, landing on their backs and started laughing.

"What a day," Yogi said.

"Yeah, what a day."

They headed out first thing in the morning and continued south along the highway. They saw a small store next to the beach. They were broke and hungry. Yogi parked in front of the store and they got off and looked inside. It was closed. Inside the window they could see a stack of Cracker Jack boxes, potato chips, and assorted candy bars.

Yogi stepped over to the bike and pulled a wrench out of the tool kit beneath the seat. He handed it to Abel. "Here," he said. "Take this and smash that window. Then grab whatever you can and hop on."

Abel gritted his teeth, looked around to see that nobody was watching, and then took the wrench. Yogi backed the bike up to the door and began revving the motor. BRRRING DING DING DING...BRRRING DING DING DING. "Go ahead. Do it!" he yelled.

BAM! Abel hit the window hard, then again harder. It shattered easily. He shoved the wrench in his back pocket, grabbed as many boxes of Cracker Jacks as he could hold, and jumped on to the back of the Honda. "Let's go!" he yelled as he tried to hold on with arms full of Cracker Jacks.

They headed down the highway and disappeared into the distance as the sound of gunshots rang out behind them. He heard a man yelling in the distance, "Come back, you little bastards!"

Abel felt the bullets whizzing by his head as he crouched lower, desperately holding on for his life. "Man, they're shooting at us. We're gonna die."

Yogi looked back and said, "Sounds like a .22. They're too far away for them to do much damage."

"*Much* damage?"

Yogi pulled onto the side road into the hills where they rode for about a quarter mile through the brush. They came to a stop and Yogi said, "We've got to dump the bike. My step-dad probably reported it stolen already, and no telling what those other bastards are going to do."

"What are *we* going to do? That's what I want to know. What the hell are *we* going to do?"

Yogi said, "Let's just hide the bike and start walking over these hills."

They hid the motorcycle under some bushes and they ran into the brush. They came to a clearing, out of breath, and took a much-needed rest, devouring their hard-earned plunder - four boxes of Cracker Jacks. Soon they heard a helicopter circling above their location and Yogi said, "Time to move on."

They hiked into the hills for about ten miles until they came out on the highway again. Then they began hitchhiking. A van full of hippies stopped and let them in. "You guys heading down as far as Vista Linda?" Yogi asked as they sat down cross-legged in the back.

The driver turned and said, "Yeah, man. We're going right past there." A longhaired hippie with a tie-dyed tee shirt took a hit off a bong and passed it Abel's way. Abel took a big drag because the smoke was smooth and cool. He tried to hold it but the smoke expanded quickly in his lungs and he began coughing uncontrollably. Everybody started laughing as Yogi grabbed the pipe out of his hand.

"I'll take this." He took a big hit and started coughing even worse than Abel did. "Damn," he said with a toothy grin, "that's some good shit."

"Panama Red," said the longhaired guy with the tie-dyed tee shirt as Yogi passed the bong to the Mexican guy sitting in the passenger seat.

Vista Linda was a college town, famous as a party town, with beautiful beaches and bronzed bikini-clad vegetarians.

The smell of incense was in the air, and something more: looks of nervous excitement replaced the usual casual smiles. They approached a large gathering of people and listened to the murmuring of the crowd.

"They just blew up the Bank of America," someone shouted.

"Down with the establishment," a woman yelled. She raised her fist above her head in the symbol of solidarity.

"Right on," Abel said, lifting his fist in the sky.

Yogi flashed a peace sign and said, "All we need is love."

The crowd grew larger and more intense. Truckloads of police, storm troopers in riot gear, with Plexiglas shields and shotguns, rumbled down the street. A deep voice echoed through a bullhorn, "Anyone on the streets after sundown will be arrested."

The western sky was red with the approaching sunset. Yogi and Abel looked at each other with lost expressions. Yogi said, "Man, we gotta get out of here."

Abel looked at his watch and shook his head. "I don't think we have enough time. They're shutting down the whole town. What are we going to do?" He paced back and forth nervously.

A brown haired girl wearing an Army jacket and headband heard them talking and looked over at them. "You guys need a place to crash?"

Abel nodded his head. "Yeah."

"There's a frat house down the street. They're always taking in runaways and street people. Come on, I'll show you."

They followed her down the block to a two-story Victorian style house with a buck-toothed guy sitting on the front porch playing the guitar. "Welcome to Alpha Omega house," he said without missing a lick. They stepped toward the door. He looked back to where the girl was standing, but she had gone. Yogi and Abel looked at each other, shrugged, and entered the house. The pungent scent of marijuana, incense, patchouli oil and sweat filled the air as the rhythms of Jimi Hendrix ripped through the house. They found a couple of beanbag chairs and made themselves at home. Someone passed a joint Abel's way and he took a big toke, holding it in his lungs for as long as he could and letting it out slowly. They smoked pot and listened as a group of radicals debated the merits of Martin Luther King and Malcolm X.

"By any means necessary," said a blonde-haired girl wearing love beads and a peace sign. She raised her fist above her head. "Off the pigs!"

"Only nonviolence can win the hearts and minds of the people," said a black man wearing a leather jacket and black beret. "Love is the answer." He pointed his index finger skyward.

The next morning Abel and Yogi stuck out their thumbs and headed farther south. They ended up in Sadoma Canyon and hung out in front of an organic food store where they panhandled and offered to work for food and a place to stay. "Spare some change, man?" Yogi said to an older dude who pulled up in a VW van.

The man slid the door open, smiled broadly, and said, "You guys need a place to stay? I need a couple of young guys to help me in the yard."

"No problem," Yogi volunteered.

"Get in," the old man chimed. The van bounced through the canyon and the radio blasted The Rolling Stone's "Sympathy for the Devil."

They arrived at a three level Spanish-style house with a red tile roof tucked deep into the hills. It was rustic, with a tile patio, Jacuzzi, sunken living room with open skylights and wide circular windows. The old man cooked steaks and brought out a bottle of expensive wine. "This is Cabernet Sauvignon," he said as he poured it into fancy wine glasses.

As the night wore on, he brought out some pot and they all got stoned. He went to the closet and brought out a couple of pillows. He tossed them on the bed. "You guys are a lot of fun." He lay down on the bed and patted the mattress. "Every summer, I

invite a few sailors up here from the base," he said
with a giggle. "Yeah, I always offer them a few bucks
to get down and dirty."

Yogi and Abel looked at each other in shock. They
laughed nervously.

"You know if you guys want to make about
twenty bucks apiece..."

Yogi stood up and pounded his fist into his palm.
"Sorry, pal," Yogi said, furrowing his brows. "That's
not our thing. We're not into that stuff. So you better
quit that talk while you're ahead."

The old man got up from the bed and said, "Hey,
I didn't really mean it. I was just making a joke." He
giggled like a little girl and backed away slowly.
"Please don't hurt me. I'll leave you alone." He
slipped out of the room and went upstairs.

Yogi lit up a joint and passed it Abel's way. "Can
you believe that joker?"

"No. We'd better lock the door or else who knows
what he might do once we go to sleep."

When they woke up the next morning, the old
man was gone. They made a bunch of toast with
butter and jelly, and then scrambled some eggs. They
sat there eating without talking, only the sounds of
birds chirping outside the window. When they
finished eating, Yogi threw his plate against the wall
and kicked over the chairs, as Abel sat there with his
arms crossed.

"OK. That's enough," Abel said.

Yogi glared at him and said, "What are you some kind of a queer lover?"

Abel stood up and shook his head. "Let's just go."

They left the house and headed back toward the highway.

They put out their thumbs and headed north on Left Coast Highway. Their second ride took them straight past Eden Valley and on up to Big Norte. Smiling people of all descriptions greeted them – dropouts from society, drug dealers on the run, ex-convicts, bikers, mystics, runaway teenagers like themselves, and a few curiosity seekers.

"You should've been here last night," one hippie with a thick New York accent, exclaimed. "These girls took us to their cabin and we all got wasted on Orange Sunshine and Red Mountain. Before we knew it, everybody was naked and we painted each other's bodies with Day-glo. It was crazy, man."

"Far out," Abel replied, nodding his head.

"Cool," said Yogi. "Where's all the dope?" He held his hands out, palms up.

Just then, a psychedelic Volkswagen pulled up. A longhaired guy wearing a dirty black top hat, flowered shirt and love beads jumped out. "The Candy Man's here," he said, and pulled out a plastic bag full of pills and started handing them out to everyone.

Strawberry double dome. LSD. Acid. They stuck out their hands and their tongues. The merry prankster gave each of them a hit of acid and they washed it down with Red Mountain Burgundy.

"Far out," Abel exclaimed as he embarked on what was probably his hundredth LSD trip. Diamonds laced the velvet night and the moon was full of light. A radio played the Beatles' "Lucy in the Sky with Diamonds" and a group of them began to dance. The moon started changing shape, turning into a silver bowl as stars interconnected with lines as graceful as a spider's web. He was one with the universe as the group joined together in a cosmic OM. The mantra permeated his being. *I am one with all that is and was and ever shall be. I AM THAT. I AM. I AM THAT I AM. OM.*

The radio began to play "Strawberry Fields Forever" and they were all dancing and making out beneath a silver shower of stars. A naked girl skipped up to Abel and took him by the hand. They started dancing and twirling and skipping around an open meadow. They ended up in the back of a '57 Chevy where she climbed on top of him and started kissing him all over.

Yogi and Abel ran into each other the next day as they recovered from their respective haze. They laughed and embraced as long lost friends. "This place is wild, man," he said.

"Man, I can barely remember what happened."

Abel sat down on a log and buried his head in his hands. The night had left them in a daze and they tried to recapture it.

The hippies passed sunflower seeds and blonde Lebanese hash in a circle around the campfire. Yogi and Abel sat down on a pair of tree stumps and joined the circle. As the hash pipe went around, each hit brought flashbacks of the previous night's adventures. Abel lost himself in multi-dimensional geometric patterns as he spat the sunflower seed shells into the fire. Glistening arcs trailed to the center of the sun. Rainbows traced their pathways as he sought hidden meaning.

Suddenly, a pair of eyes full of racial hatred stared at Abel. A big biker with long matted black hair and a bushy beard stood over him and stared as silence overcame him. He gasped in fear, a sunflower seed stuck in his throat, and he started choking. Gasping for breath, he tried to cough in order to dislodge the shell from his throat. He imagined the shell entering his lungs. He thought, *This the birth of my death*, choking to his doom as Fear wrapped its icy fingers around his throat in a fierce embrace.

Abel looked up and the man with the evil stare was gone. Perhaps he was just a phantom in the night, nonexistent. His thoughts wandered to familiar territory, *I am alone, embraced by a lake of loneliness, a lost soul, lost in loneliness.* He coughed again and the sunflower shell spiraled through the air in a trail of stars.

After days of partying Yogi said, "Let's move on," and they grabbed their packs and headed toward the road. They looked up and down the long, winding Left Coast Highway and then looked at each other.

"What way do we go?" Abel asked.

"It's getting boring up here. Let's head back down to Vista Linda again where the action is." They thumbed their way back down south.

Once again, the highway took them straight past Eden Valley. They looked at each other without comment, yet Abel felt a tug at his heart begging him to go home. *My parents are probably worried sick and I don't even know why I left.*

Their ride stopped and let them out about thirty miles north of Vista Linda. They stuck out their thumbs again and watched the cars whiz by one-by-one. They made a game of it by making faces and begging on their knees as the cars approached. Finally, one stopped – a black and white Dodge Coronet. Abel punched at the air.

The doors with the words California Highway Patrol emblazoned on the sides within their bright gold shield opened. He thought, *Nowhere to run. It's over.* He started biting his fingernails. Two CHP officers stepped out of the car. Yogi and Abel just stood there waiting for the inevitable. One of the officers came toward them and said, "You boys got ID?"

Yogi dug his hands in his pockets and shrugged his shoulders. "I must have lost mine."

"Me too."

"You boys look like runaways. You're going to come with us. Get in." The other officer opened the back door of the Dodge and they got in.

They took them to the local substation and put them in a holding cell. After about an hour another officer, an older man with all kinds of badges and stripes on his uniform, opened the door and said, "OK, boys, I'm going to give you two choices. You can both give me your names and tell us where you're from, or you can go to Juvenile Hall.

Abel stood up and approached him. He looked at Yogi and shook his head, then turned to the officer and said, "Alright, my name is Abel Adams and my parents are in Eden Valley. I'm ready to go home." He looked down at the floor.

The officer looked over at Yogi. "What about you, young man?"

Yogi just sat there and folded his arms. "Go ahead. Take me to the hall." The officer let Abel out of the holding cell and closed the door behind him as Yogi sat there sullenly.

Abel gave the officer his home number and he called his parents. He looked over at him and asked, "Do you want to talk to them?"

He shook his head and looked away. He sat there and waited for about two hours. They finally showed up and his mom came over to hug him. "We were so worried about you." He stood there with his arms by his sides as she wrapped her arms around him and wept.

***

Abel's relationship with his parents steadily declined to the point where they would hardly ever speak to each other. He stayed away from home as much as possible, smoking marijuana and tripping out on LSD and wine.

He started selling marijuana to support his growing drug habit. Commercial weed was going for ten dollars an ounce. He bought a pound for about $90 and after taking out a couple of ounces for himself, he still wound up with about $50 profit per pound. What he liked more than the money was the feeling of acceptance. Everybody wanted to be his friend. He had what they wanted.

His enterprise nearly came to a screeching halt when he returned home to discover his stash – four ounces of Korean Green – was missing from his closet. That was forty dollars worth. He took care of his deficit immediately by sneaking up to his parent's room and stealing forty dollars from his dad's wallet, which he still left on top of the dresser.

He went back to his room to think about his next move. Suddenly he looked up and saw his father standing there in the doorway with his arms folded across his chest. "What happened to the money that was on the dresser?"

Abel hung his head. "I needed it to pay back this guy who was letting me hold onto something that belonged to him."

His father took a deep breath and sighed. "Don't you know you could go to jail for having that crap in the house?"

"But it wasn't mine. I was just holding it for this guy and I need to give it back to him. Where is it? I'll just take it over to him right now and get rid of it."

"It's gone. I burned it." His father stuck his hands in his pockets and turned to walk away.

Abel lifted his hands to his head in disbelief. "Aw, man."

His father stopped and turned toward him. "And you're grounded for a month." Then he walked out of the room.

"Aw, man." He kicked the trashcan across the room.

By this time, he was too big for them to hit anymore. He was taller than both of his parents were, and they knew he would probably hit back.

The phone rang and he picked it up. It was Jay. He told him that Keisha was in the hospital with sickle cell anemia. She had been calling him for a long time and he had not responded to her calls. He finally gave in and went to visit her. He brought her some fake flowers and a couple of tacos from Jack in the Box.

Keisha's crisis subsided and the doctor released her from the hospital the next day. She was sitting on the bus when Abel got on, but he avoided eye contact and went to sit in the back.

He got high and hitchhiked to Reston Beach to see Jasmine. She missed him. She wanted to smother him with love. He couldn't take too much of it. He had to get away from her after a few hours.

A few days later, one of Keisha's friends came up to him and said, "She back in the hospital again. She wants you to go see her." This time he didn't go to see her. He didn't want to think about her. He refused her calls. She died a week later and he felt like he had killed her by not loving her.

He took two tabs of Orange Sunshine, grabbed his notebook, and hitchhiked to Free Beach. He was alone. He took off all his clothes and listened to the sounds of the sea. He wrote…

These are words
Which came to me
While sitting by the silver sea
As lightning danced upon the waves
And thunder echoed in the caves.

This is that which must be done
Before the setting of the sun
Unraveling the mysteries
Conceived in ancient histories.

This is it
And these are they
Revealed to only those who pray.
Sound the trumpets.

Pound the drums
For revelation now to come.
Words as these
Unveiled in verse
The secrets of the universe
As chariots of purple flame
Race to a destiny, unnamed.

CHAPTER 4

JESUS FREAKS

✳

The big red and white tent billowed in stark contrast to the drab stucco building that housed the county methadone clinic across the park. Longhaired hippie musicians played Christian rock and roll. Jesus Freaks.

Abel, Yogi, Max, and Jay Hanuman decided to check it out after school. First, they stopped to smoke a couple of joints. After getting stoned, they headed toward the tent.

The music sounded like Crosby, Stills, Nash and Young. He couldn't tell the Jesus Freaks from the hippies and the dopers. Abel was so stoned that he barely paid attention to the people who were coming forward and giving testimonies. The Reverend was telling everyone how Jesus loved them. How He died and rose again from the grave. Finally, he gave an invitation for people to come forward and accept

Jesus Christ as Lord and Savior. Abel folded his arms across his chest.

He recognized several people that he knew in the audience. Several of them were going forward to accept Christ. Jay's sister, Grace, was there. She looked over at Abel and waved. As Abel started to walk toward her, Yogi pulled out a joint and invited the guys outside to get high. They left together and got stoned.

***

Abel's father was appointed chair of the physics department and his family had a new home custom built in an upper crust area of Eden Valley called Lake Eden Estates.

Abel's parents met another black professional couple who also lived in Lake Eden Estates. Ed Gaines was a doctor. His wife Nancy was a stay-at-home mom. They had a son, Randy, who was the same age as Abel and liked to get high.

Abel and Randy were hanging out in a shopping center when a young brother with long black dreadlocks like a Rastafarian approached. "What's happening, man?" he greeted them. He was darker than crude oil and his eyes were black and glowing. Abel figured he was grooving on some good acid. He reminded Abel of a prophet.

"How's it going?" Abel responded. Abel was hoping he wanted to get them high.

"Have you seen the Light?" he asked.

"Let's get out of here," Randy begged. There was a pained look on his face.

"It's cool, man," Abel replied. He figured they had nothing better to do. Abel turned to the Prophet and said, "Yeah, I've got a light." He pulled out a cigarette lighter and flicked it into a small yellow flame.

Randy shook his head and sighed. Abel was silent as he flicked the lighter closed and put it back in his pocket.

The Prophet continued. There was a sense of urgency to his voice. "Have you seen the Light?"

"What Light?" Abel grew weary of his probing.

There was thunder echoing in the distance and the clouds began to darken. The sky threatened rain.

"Look to the Light within," the Prophet said extending his finger toward his heart. He looked Abel in the eye intently. "The first step to peace is to stand still in the Light. Be still and know."

"Who are you?" Abel asked.

The darkness from the clouds began to vanish and the light shone through in heavenly shafts of gold. Abel looked at the Prophet for a moment and he could see something in his eyes like the scintilla of ten thousand stars.

Randy grabbed Abel by the arm. "Let's go."

Abel looked at the Prophet and shook his head sadly. As he turned to walk away, he heard the Prophet say, "Remember…the Light is within you and all around you."

Lighting flashed, followed by an echo of thunder. Abel looked back and the Prophet was gone. It began to rain and they ran for cover. They ran to Randy's BMW and headed across town, blasting the sounds of "Ramble On" by Led Zeppelin.

Randy handed Abel a joint when they got in and they got stoned on the way home. They talked about the recent deaths of Jimi Hendrix, Janis Joplin and Jim Morrison.

CHAPTER 5

BAD REPUTATION

✳

Abel soon established a reputation in school for being a cool doper who was usually stoned on acid and who always had good weed. He was going out to Los Tecatos every week to pick up ten to twenty kilos for about $120 each. He would usually buy one or two for himself and break it down into quarter pounds and ounces. Although he was sure that his parents knew what was going on, they seemed helpless to do anything about it. He was out of control. At age sixteen, he was going out with several different girls, dealing dope, staying high and going to parties almost every night. Most of his friends were white.

One of Abel's girlfriends was Hillary Raincross, whose father was Judge Jeffrey Raincross. "Jeffrey," as she called him, was cool when Abel would come over to visit, knowing that his father was a respected professor. Hillary's mother, on the other hand, was on the local school board and made no effort to disguise her disapproval of her innocent young daughter's relationship with a young black man.

Sometimes Hillary and Abel would sit in front of the school and make out on the front lawn. Her mother got wind of this and soon there was a new rule prohibiting students from sitting or loitering on the lawns in front of the school. No problem. They just took their activities elsewhere.

Once when his parents were out of town at a conference, Abel invited everyone over for a party. Their house had an indoor pool and a Jacuzzi so as soon as the girls arrived they all just got naked and went skinny-dipping. There was plenty of alcohol, marijuana, assorted psychedelics and pharmaceuticals. One girl threw up on the rug and passed out. She woke up to discover Yogi's hand down her pants. That sobered her up enough to get dressed and find her way home.

Hillary and Abel went upstairs to his parent's bedroom while everyone else continued partying downstairs in the living room and in the pool. Drunken Cindy Summers interrupted them and insisted on joining them in a threesome.

Hillary's mother threatened to send her to rehab if she kept seeing Abel. Two months later Hillary's mother kept her promise and sent her to a residential treatment center in Cornerstone.

The parties continued almost non-stop throughout his sophomore year in high school. He got a summer job in the vineyards of Los Tecatos working with Jay Hanuman. They became good friends, sharing similar tastes in wine, weed, and women. With the money he made working and selling marijuana he was able to go into the business of dealing mescaline, a psychedelic powder made from the extract of the peyote cactus. Usually, it turned out to be LSD mixed with Nestlé's Quick.

He sold about twenty caps of "mescaline" a day at school and even more on the weekends. Abel and his friends partied in the mountains and everybody liked to get totally wasted on psychedelics and wine.

They spent long hours after school hanging out in the trailer behind Jay's mother's house drinking beer, smoking weed and tripping on LSD. Occasionally they indulged in sniffing spray paint or gasoline and anything else that would give them another way of looking at reality. Jay started getting weird, talking about the devil and demons as if he knew of them from first-hand experience. Sometimes he would just start laughing for no reason. Other times he would get upset at everyone and start cursing about how everyone was against him.

Jay was giving a party at his mom's house. She was gone for the weekend. The party was for Yogi, who had just gotten out of jail. Yogi had tattoos down both arms, wore sunglasses at night and had a goatee that made him look like a jazz musician. He had just finished doing a year in reform school for multiple assaults and drug possession. Judge Jeffrey Raincross handed Yogi the sentence, calling him "a menace to society."

The pungent aroma of pot and patchouli oil filled the air as Rod Stewart's latest album played in the background. Max played his guitar and sang along in the background. Abel became fascinated with Jay's younger sister, Grace. Her soft amber eyes and sandy brown hair reflected innocence. He kept on replaying the song, "Someone Like You" and singing along with it until Grace consented to follow him into the nearest empty bedroom. Abel shut the door behind them as her brother Jay fumed silently. They kissed gently and Abel tried to reach under her blouse. "No," she said, grabbing his hand. "I'm a Christian and I'm saving myself until I get married."

Abel pulled his hand away and gazed into her eyes longingly. Grace smiled and held his hand. "I think you're a very special man, beautiful, wonderful. But this path you're on." She paused and bit her lip, looking away for a moment.

Abel held her hands to his lips, kissing them gently. "You're the one who's special. I've never met anyone like you before. All the girls I know, they just want to get high and have sex. I know this sounds crazy, because that's where I'm at right now, but sometimes I think that one day I'll settle down with someone like you." The Rod Stewart song played softly in the background. "I'm just not ready for that right now. I've gotta do my thing," he said as he stood up.

Grace reached for him and pulled him back to her. "Just one more thing. Please pray with me."

Abel pulled away and turned toward the door. "Maybe some other time," he said.

Abel opened the door and Jay was standing there, obviously upset. He was also quite drunk. "What the heck are you doing?" he slurred as he tried to push him away.

"Back off, punk!" Abel replied.

"Damn you, Abel," Jay snarled, eyes half-closed.

Abel hit him with a right hook, knocking him back against the wall. Max stepped in to defend Jay and Abel backhanded him across the face. Jay tried to grab Abel from behind and Yogi came to his rescue. Within minutes, everyone joined the fight and nearly destroyed the house. The night became a blur of fists, bottles, flying chairs, girls screaming, and people running in all directions. "It's a mad house!" Abel shouted in his best Charlton Heston impression.

Abel went home and thought about Grace. His head reeled from alcohol and marijuana, but through the blur, he managed to find his notebook and began to write a poem about her.

> *You'll always be a part of me*
> *In spite of distant miles*
> *Through time and space illusion*
> *I'll be thinking of your smile*
> *And even in the darkest hours*

Long before the dawn
You'll always be a part of me
Like sunlight on the sea.
I always will remember you
No matter where you go
In spite of all our differences
I'll always love you so
And even in the hours of darkness
Long before the dawn
You'll always be a part of me
Like sunlight on the sea.

I'll always be here loving you
No matter what they say
The teardrops spent on missing you
Are not too much to pay
And even in the hours of darkness
Long before the dawn
You'll always be a part of me
A precious part of me.

Like sunlight in the sea
You are a precious part of me
Like dewdrops on the ground
Our hearts are one
And always will be
And even in the hours of darkness
Long before the dawn of springtime
I'll always be here loving you.

As Abel wrote the final line, he passed out and dreamed he was a butterfly.

***

The next morning they all got back together and exchanged versions. Jay clearly came out as the loser, even though he was the one who started everything. They made up quickly over a gallon of Red Mountain Burgundy, an ounce of home grown, and a few choruses of Led Zeppelin's "Whole Lotta Love." Abel's parents were gone for the afternoon so he invited the guys over to go swimming.

Yogi and Abel stayed up all night zapped out of their minds on speed. The next morning they were crashing heavy when Randy Gaines stopped by and invited them to drive up the coast to Big Norte for the day. His parents had let him borrow their BMW for the day. It sounded like an excellent idea at the time.

They headed up the coast, fired up a joint of Korean Green, and listened to the Beatles song, "With a Little Help from our Friends." They arrived in Big Norte at around 2:00 p.m. and Abel immediately set off to score them some acid. He found a guy selling blotter acid with pictures of Mr. Natural, a long legged old hippie character from Zap Comix. He bought three hits and brought them back to Randy and Yogi.

"What's this?" Randy asked. He looked at the tiny blotter with a confused expression on his face.

"Don't tell me you've never done blotter acid?" Abel sighed.

"What do I do with it?" He was seriously lame about it.

Yogi and Abel looked at each other and laughed. Abel could tell this was going to be a silly day.

"Drop it," Yogi said.

Randy opened his hand and let the paper fall from his hand.

"No, stupid. I mean take it." He picked up the tiny LSD-soaked square and handed it back to him. "Like this," he demonstrated, placing the paper on his tongue.

Yogi did likewise. Randy hesitated for a moment then followed suit.

"Now give it about twenty or thirty minutes to kick in," he said. "This is supposed to be some powerful stuff."

"Groovy," Randy replied, smiling like a child.

"Let's go look for some chicks," Yogi suggested.

"Cool," Abel replied. "Let's go for it."

"Alright," Randy intoned.

"Party time," Abel yelled. They were ready for action.

They joined hands in the middle like the three musketeers and let out a rebel yell.

Zap City. Electric Avenue. The acid beamed its magic through their brains and they were walking in space. They laughed hysterically as they wandered into a health food restaurant. It was hard to sit still after awhile so they decided it was time to get out of there.

They got in the car and Randy started down the Left Coast Highway. The BMW became one with the curving lines in the road as the acid flowed through their brains and they exploded into cosmic consciousness. Jefferson Airplane was playing "White Rabbit" on the stereo and Abel started tripping into deep space. Cosmic void beckoned him into the darkness of her womb. Heavy. Abel's stomach tightened and the arms of loneliness embraced him. The Three Assassins, Guilt, Fear, and Resentment, attacked.

Guilt stabbed Abel in the back with a silver dagger. Fear strangled him with a hangman's rope as Resentment injected his deadly poison into his veins. He screamed, "Let me out of here!"

Randy was lost in the music and the rhythm of the road, flying around each curve in his magnificent winged chariot. The chariot continued racing down the coast highway as his panic overwhelmed him. He looked out at the ocean and felt it calling him home. Siren song. Yogi was playing it cool, engrossed in nature's scenery, smoking a joint and grooving to the music. Abel had to get out of there. He was ready to jump out the window and he said so.

"Let me out of here, now!" Abel shouted.

"Okay, okay," Randy replied, finally taking him seriously. He slowed to a stop along the side of the road as he dove out into the street, terrified. Deep from the bottom of his soul, anger raged like a volcano, suddenly coming to life. He was full into fight or flight.

Everyone was out to get him. Paranoia filled his brain like an ice bucket and he ran screaming toward an oncoming car.

"I can't take it anymore," he raved. "I'm out of here."

Zoom! A speeding car fish tailed as the driver hit the brakes, narrowly avoiding him and almost diving off the cliff.

Another driver cursed Abel as he skidded to a stop in front of him. The driver wheeled around Abel slowly and gave him the finger.

Yogi grabbed Abel and pulled him out of the road. Abel broke away from him swinging wildly and ran to the side of the cliff. He was ready to jump.

"Don't do it!" Yogi screamed.

"Abel," yelled Randy.

Abel jumped headlong into the Abyss, freefalling into the wide-open jaws of death. Cosmic void calling him home.

Then he woke up. He was in a hospital, under observation. Miraculously, he only suffered a few small cuts. Someone was watching out for him.

For He shall give his angels charge over thee to keep thee in all thy ways; they shall bear thee up in their hands, lest thou dash thy foot against a stone.

CHAPTER 6

HEAVEN

*

Abel continued getting high and dealing. Although marijuana was his main staple, psychedelics were the spice of his life. He sold mescaline to everyone on campus. He didn't care if he knew them or not, as long as they looked cool. He carried his stash in a metal Sucrets case that he hid in his coat pocket. He did most of his dealing during the breaks between classes.

Abel didn't suspect a thing when Cindy Summers approached him. She asked him, "Are you holding?"

He took a furtive glance over his shoulder. "What are you looking for?"

"Mescaline. Two tabs. How much?"

"Three bucks each or two for five."

She handed Abel a five-dollar bill and he stuffed it into his pants pocket. He looked around to make sure they weren't being watched and then he took out the Sucrets case. He opened it and took out two capsules of the brown powder.

"Thanks, a lot," she said with a nervous smile. She put the capsules in her purse and looked over her shoulder.

"It's good stuff," he said as she was leaving.

An hour later, he was walking down the hallway on his way to his next class. That was when he saw two men in dark suits. He recognized one of the men as Mr. Fowler, the Dean of Students. The other man he had never seen before. They both seemed to know who he was. Before he could change directions, they approached him and grabbed him by the arms. "Abel Adams, would you mind coming with us?"

Abel stuck his hand in his coat pocket and felt the Sucrets case. It probably contained about 20 caps of mescaline. They escorted him into the office and told him to sit down. As he did so, he deftly slid the Sucrets case behind him under the seat cushion of the chair.

"I'm Lieutenant Mendoza of the Eden County Narcotics Task Force, and I'd like to ask you a few questions," he began.

The Dean excused himself and left the room. It was just Abel and the Lieutenant. "What do you want?" Abel asked. He stood up defiantly.

"How much money do you have on you?" the Lieutenant asked.

"Heck, don't know. A few bucks, maybe. Why?"

"Would you mind emptying your pockets?"

"Yeah, I do mind. But here, I'll do it anyway," he responded. He pulled out a wad of bills and placed them on the desk in front of him.

"Is that all of it?" he asked.

He reached into both pockets and pulled out a couple of more wads of crumpled up bills. Then he reached back in, grabbed a couple of handfuls of change, and dropped them on the desk in a pile. The Lieutenant began sorting through the bills, examining each one carefully. He must have been looking for a particular mark or serial number because when he came across the five-dollar bill, he wrote something down in a little notebook and put it in a plastic envelope.

"So what are you doing, taking my money?" Abel demanded.

"You'll get your money back."

"I want it back now."

"Go ahead. Pick it up."

Abel grabbed the rest of his money from the desktop, minus the five-dollar bill, and stuffed it back into his pockets. He sat back down. While the Lieutenant was busy putting the plastic envelope in his briefcase and filling out a few forms, he grabbed the Sucrets box from under the seat cushion and put it back in his coat pocket. The Lieutenant snapped his briefcase shut and stood to his feet. Abel stood up and glanced at the door.

"Abel Adams," he said, "I'm arresting you for sale of dangerous drugs." He reached for his handcuffs.

"No way!" Abel shouted as he bolted out the door and ran out of the office. He ran down the bleachers and tossed the Sucrets case into the bushes. He kept running until he got off school property.

As soon as he ran across the street two cop cars screeched to a halt in front of him. The cops jumped out with their guns drawn and Abel put his hands in the air.

The cops transported Abel to juvenile hall and put him in twenty-four hour isolation. The cell was about five by seven with a metal toilet, a metal sink, a metal bed, and a small metal table. He cried himself to sleep.

The next day he entered general population and met some of the other juvenile offenders. Several kids were there for runaway and out of control. Others, like him, were there for crimes ranging from burglary to murder. Still others were there because they had no place else to go. Many had come from sexually and physically abusive households. Others had simply been abandoned and neglected and were awaiting placement in foster care.

The Public Defender showed Abel a copy of the police report. It described in detail how narcs busted Cindy Summers for possession of dangerous drugs and made a deal with her to set up one of the campus connections. "That rat," Abel muttered as he read the report. Originally, she was supposed to set up Jay Hanuman, but she saw Abel first.

Judge Raincross sentenced Abel to Los Perdidos Boy's Camp for an indeterminate term. The program normally lasted about six months to a year, but he could be released early if he participated in counseling and did well in school.

Los Perdidos was located in the hills about 50 miles north of Eden Valley. The main compound consisted of a large dormitory, kitchen, dining area, and recreation area. They were required to attend school five days a week, through a cooperative program with Los Osos High School. The school was just a brisk morning walk up the hill along the Z - Trail.

They shaved his head and gave him a set of camp uniforms consisting of jeans, T-shirts, Khaki work shirts and a brown cloth jacket. He felt like a real convict.

The staff divided the boys into several groups called Tribes. Each tribe had it own counselor. In his spare time, he lifted weights, read inspirational self-help books, and hung out with the homeboys. He learned about burglary, forgery and armed robbery.

Abel did his best to get out of camp as soon as possible. He became a model student, studying hard and doing extra credit work whenever possible. He went in as a junior and came out four months later as a high school graduate.

Abel got out of camp a week after his seventeenth birthday. He had become a different person. Instead of being a hippie and a doper, he now identified himself as a criminal. He was a drug dealer with visions of grandeur who visualized himself as a multimillionaire crime lord with his own private island.

He spent the next few weeks partying with the old gang. Not much had changed. Yogi Santana had just gotten out of jail again for heroin possession. They were sitting around in the trailer one hot afternoon when they decided it was time to get a little higher. Jay suggested they buy some heroin. He had tried it a couple of times before and said that it was beyond anything they had ever tried.

They went in together on a dime. Yogi scored for them from a junkie out in Los Tecatos. He also brought them three sets of works consisting of a needle and syringe along with a spoon or bottle cap to cook the dope in. A glass of water was on the table. Yogi emptied the brownish powder into a measuring spoon and drew up one cc of water into the syringe. He squirted the water onto the powder carefully and held the spoon over a candle flame. They watched in trance-like fascination as the liquid flashed to a boil, casting off a deep aroma of something magic. He took apart a cigarette filter and set a tiny piece of the cotton in the center of the brown liquid. "The cotton is like a filter," he said. "It strains out the impurities."

Slowly and methodically, they filled their syringes with the amber solution. Yogi went first. He tied himself off with a belt and the blue vein in the pit of his elbow bulged. He tapped the needle in gently and drew back on the plunger. A scarlet thread of blood filled the syringe and he loosened the tie. Then he pressed down on the plunger, emptying the dark liquid into his arm. His reaction was immediate. His eyelids drooped; he scratched his nose, and smiled. "Whoa, man," he slurred. "This is some good junk."

"Alright," Jay exclaimed. He took the belt and tied it around his bicep as he prepared the next fix. Smacked back to the max, his eyelids drooped as he lit a cigarette and let it hang from the corner of his mouth like James Dean.

Abel's turn. He held his breath as he tapped the needle against the pit of his elbow piercing the vein as the scarlet thread quickly filled the syringe. Boom! It hit him in the pit of the stomach with a warm rush throughout his body like an orgasm of peace and safety. He was walking in space surrounded by webs of soft cotton. He had returned to the womb. He knew this was the paradise from which he was exiled so long ago. Now, having seized the flaming sword, he conquered the angel of the gate and returned to his Eden. He slowly pulled the needle from his arm and dropped it into the glass of water on the table. "Heaven," Abel whispered. "This is what heaven must be like." He looked at himself in the mirror and saw eyes. Beautiful eyes. He was beautiful. Perfect. The poppy hadn't made him crazy after all. It had given him back his sanity. This was that which he had long sought. This was that.

He knew then what Yogi had meant when he had said to him just a couple of years back, "I think I'll become a junkie. Then I'll only have one problem to worry about." The words echoed in his brain as he slowly sank into bliss.

He found the answers to the questions which, when pondered, would lead to enlightenment. He knew at that moment what his life would be about. He would become a junkie. Then he'd only have one problem to worry about.

Heroin was the perfect drug for relieving his primal pain. It penetrated every level of his being, down to the core of his soul. Deep within him was a pain that traced its way all the way back to his birth and perhaps beyond. It was the pain of separation, the original hurt, an itch that, until now, he could not even begin to scratch. Just like the Demerol that swept through his blood as he was being born, this heroin exorcised all tension and distress from his soul and he was once again at one with the universe. *Peace with God. Atonement. At-one-ment. I AM THAT. We are one.*

He pledged unwavering fealty to his new lord and master, King Heroin. All other loyalties and ambitions had to be broken like so many clay idols before the all-consuming fire of ritual sacrifice. He was now willing to go to any lengths to maintain this bliss. Losing sight of his few remaining values, he spent all the money he had saved through dealing and working in the vineyards. After he had sold most of his own valuable possessions, he began stealing from his parents.

In 1973 the heroin was potent and inexpensive. Abel, Jay, and Yogi would drive out to Los Tecatos and score thirty-dollar balloons of the brown powder, which was enough to keep three people loaded all day. The dope was wrapped in balloons to make it easier to swallow if they got pulled over by the cops. A thirty-dollar balloon could be divided into about five dimes or ten nickels. A nickel was enough to get two people high. Once you developed a habit, however, your tolerance would increase, and they knew a few guys who could shoot up a whole thirty-dollar bag at one time.

The summer of 1973 was a blur of narcotic bliss intermingled with stolen ten speeds, tape decks and treachery. Abel worked in the vineyards again for a while and started selling heroin to support his growing habit. He had finally found his place in life. He was home again.

CHAPTER 7

ROOTS

✳

Mystic rhythms
Heartbeats
Pounding to African rhythms
Pentacostal hallelujahs
Drumbeats
Sounding to souls
Forgotten dreams
Divine remembrance
Sacred moments
Flames
Igniting loins
Long since silent
Now longing
With songs
From ancient days
Rocking with mystic rhythms
Rock hard
Entwining spirals
Dancing

Mystic rhythms
Pounding to drumbeats
Heartbeats
Pounding to memories
Sounding to centuries
Singing, clapping
Bones to stones
Laughing
Dancing in darkness
Till night gone home
Dancing in darkness
Till night gone home
Heartbeats to drumbeats
Dancing to mystic rhythms
Till night gone home

The party ended abruptly when Abel's parents decided to send him to Maryland to spend the rest of the summer with relatives. He was shipped off to the home of his mother's sister Justine and her husband Bob. Abel was supposed to get back in touch with his black cultural roots. His cousin Frank was two years older than he was and home for the summer after his first year at Banneker, the college his parents, aunts and uncles had attended.

Since Abel graduated from high school a year early, his family suggested that he was a good candidate for Banneker. They knew people on the board and said he could still enroll for the upcoming fall semester. Uncle Bob tossed Abel a catalog and told him to pick a major. Flipping through the pages, he decided on Political Science, thinking that perhaps a career in jurisprudence might be interesting. After all, he already had experience with the juvenile justice system.

Abel suffered the pains of withdrawal symptoms for the first three days he was in Maryland. He told everybody that he had the flu. Afterwards Frank took him out partying, stoned again on Strawberry Hill and Panama Red. He learned to talk, walk, dance and act black. Having lived most of his life in a predominately-white upper class, small town suburban environment, he had a hard time adjusting to this strange new culture. He felt out of place being around other blacks and he ended up suffering as much rejection from his own folks as he had from people of other races. He would be in a roomful of black people and feel so very alone. He was different. He didn't like that. He could hear their whispers. Feel their stares. They were watching him and wondering why he was the way he was. He hated himself to the core of his African roots. He hated himself for not being black enough to be considered a real black guy. He heard the whispers as he walked through the campus:

"Oreo. Black on the outside, white on the inside."

"Uncle Tom."

"Light, bright, damned near white."

"High yellow brother."

"He think he too good for us with his proper talking self."

Abel moved into the dorm and spent the first day with Frank who showed him around the campus and introduced him to his group of friends. They smoked weed and drank wine to break the ice and celebrate the coming semester.

"You know, there's three women here for every man." Frank said.

"Hey, I'm sure gonna get my three," Abel replied giving him a high five. They all busted up laughing.

Abel got back to his room that evening and finished unpacking. His new roommate was lying on his bed passed out.

The roommate came to and introduced himself, obviously intoxicated.

"What's happenin', bro," he slurred.

"You got it my man," he replied. He was getting the lingo down.

"What's your name?" he asked.

"Abel," he said, smiling.

"I'm Rico," he smiled and extended his hand. "That's short for Ricardo."

Rico murmured something that Abel couldn't understand.

"Say what?" he asked.

Rico mumbled again.

"I can't hear what you're sayin' man."

Rico sat up on his bed and pulled out a joint.

"I said… Do you get high?"

This time Abel heard him loud and clear. "Oh, yeah, man," he said offering him a light.

The grass was potent, leaving both of them so stoned they couldn't communicate. Instead, they just turned on the stereo and listened to the Funkadelics.

***

Classes began and Abel wrote his first term paper on Communism. He wrote about dialectical materialism and the ultimate fate of the capitalist state. He became fascinated with the principles and practices of revolution and participated in marches and demonstrations against The Man. Abel became a radical. He managed to keep a 3.6 average for the first semester in spite of the fact that he was getting high every night. Nobody believed that he had ever used heroin before or that he had been to juvenile hall for sales of dangerous drugs. He was a little disappointed that they perceived him as such a square and was determined to convince his new peers that he was cool and that he belonged. He wanted to fit in, desperately.

Abel came home for Christmas break and his family was proud of him. They could hardly believe that he had gotten a 3.6 average. He hadn't done that well since junior high.

While Abel was in Eden Valley, he met up with Yogi. Heroin still had the same effect on him as before. This time, however, it didn't take as long to start developing a habit. After three straight days of fixing, he could already tell that he was getting hooked again. Abel decided to back off some and stuck with pot and alcohol. He also decided to score a little quantity of herb while he was in California, so he could make some money when he got back to school.

Abel scored a pound of Columbian for $100. He carefully wrapped the weed in two layers of plastic. He soaked some rags in cologne and placed them between the bags. Then he sprinkled them with pepper and wrapped everything again. That was to keep the dogs from picking up the scent. The final package was shoved into the bottom of his dirty clothes bag and locked in a footlocker. He sent the locker back to Banneker ahead of him via Greyhound.

When he arrived in Maryland his package was waiting for him safe and sound. No problems. Everyone was impressed by Abel's daring and finesse and word soon spread throughout campus that he was the man to see for California grass.

Abel's roommate Rico was an ex-gangster from Atlanta who gave him a book called *Pimp* by Iceberg Slim. He told Abel to memorize it.

"This is your Bible," Rico said as he handed him the novel on the glories of pimping and pandering. "It will show you how a real man treats his women."

Abel read it over slowly and began to adopt a new identity. Cool Breeze, the Player, Gangster, Pimp, Dope Dealing Mac Daddy from the West Coast. He dressed the part. Silk suits, bright patterned shirts and gold chains. Platform shoes and bell-bottoms were in and he played them to the max.

As the school year ended, Abel had a pocketful of money from selling marijuana.

CHAPTER 8

UNDER THE INFLUENCE

✴

Loving you
It seems
Completes my soul
With wings
My heart takes flight
Above the limits of the lonely night

My love has wings
As angels sing
My heart takes mystic flight
Above the limits of the lonely night

Loving you
So deep
I dream of you
In sleep
And I awaken to the sun

And we are one

My love has wings
As angels sing
My heart takes mystic flight
Above the limits of the lonely night

Summer came and days blurred in the spoon of forgetfulness, as Abel listened to The Cream play "Spoonful," nodding, chasing cigarettes and drinking ice water.

Yogi, Jay and Abel soon hooked up for a spree of burglaries. They specialized in neighborhoods with names like Lakewood, Country Club, and Eden Valley Estates. The latter was Abel's own neighborhood. It didn't matter, though, because they were invincible, invisible. They always started the day by casing various neighborhoods and checking out homes where it looked like the people were on vacation. Lots of newspapers. Grass unkempt. They took note, went and got loaded, and came back when the sun went down.

Next step was to make sure nobody was home. Abel drove by the house in his mom's station wagon and checked it out visually. Then he'd park around the corner and one of them would go up to the door and ring the bell. If somebody answered, they would pretend to be looking for someone else. If nobody answered, they'd head around to the back yard and start checking windows. If nothing was unlocked, they would just pry open a window or sliding glass door with a big screwdriver. On rare occasions, they would have to break a window to get in.

The bedroom was always the first place they would check, looking through nightstands, dressers, under pillows, mattresses and closets for guns, cash, jewelry, cameras, TV's, stereos. Then they'd hit the living room and other bedrooms for coin collections, more TV's, silverware, anything of value. Boom. Gone.

They would stuff their pockets with the small stuff, fill pillowcases and pile the big stuff in a corner next to the front yard. Then Abel would run back to the car, pull it into the driveway with the lights off and they'd load her up. Then screech! Out of there.

They'd find some place to divide the loot. Most of the stuff they would just trade straight across for dope. Sometimes they would have to sell stuff for ten or twenty percent of its value. An average house would lose about ten thousand dollars worth of merchandise. They would usually end up with about five hundred dollars worth of dope, which would last them about a week.

They hit a home in Lakewood Estates. It was just before Christmas and they made a big haul. They just loaded all the presents under the tree into the back of his mom's station wagon and headed on their merry way. Before leaving Abel went through the roll top desk in the living room. Above it was a framed certificate identifying the homeowner as the

Honorable Judge Jeffrey Raincross. They had just burglarized the home of a superior court judge, the father of his ex-girlfriend Hillary. "Merry Christmas, sucker," Yogi yelled as they peeled off around the corner.

They sped off to divide the loot.

They screeched into the alley behind Yogi's pad. Making sure the coast was clear; they headed into the house with pillowcases full of stolen property. A girl with long blonde hair was sitting on the couch, smoking a cigarette. Yogi pointed to her and said, "This is Lola."

Lola was the most beautiful and seductive woman Abel had ever seen. Ice blue eyes, long silken blonde hair that hinted of Flex Balsam Shampoo. Lola quickly captured his imagination and his heart. He couldn't understand how she could be a junkie. She was too beautiful.

Abel was eighteen. Lola was twenty-one and twice the dope fiend he could ever hope to be. She had come to Yogi's that night to settle an outstanding debt.

They all got down together. Smacked back to the max. They nodded, scratched and talked philosophy over a couple of six packs of Rainier Ale.

Lola and her sister Leslie were mirror twins. Lola was right handed. Leslie was left handed. Lola was near sighted. Leslie was far sighted. Lola was thin. Leslie was on the heavy side. Lola was an anorexic, stone cold heroin addict. Leslie was a fat, raging alcoholic. Their father was an astrologer. Their mother was a neurotic.

Lola went with him to the drive-in that night and they sat in the car fixing dope, smoking pot, drinking Rainier Ale and making out. The windows were so steamed up that they never even saw what the movie was about.

Abel took Lola home and she invited him inside. "My mother is upstairs sleeping," she whispered mischievously.

She guided him through the darkened living room to the couch and let her dress fall to the floor. "Take off all your clothes," she whispered.

Moments later, they heard the creaking of the stairs and the familiar voice. "Lola, what the hell is going on down here," her mother demanded. Quickly, he scrambled into the bathroom naked as Lola tried to cover herself. His clothes were still strewn across the floor. He could hear them arguing in the living room.

"Tramp."

"Just because you never have any fun," Lola countered.

Lola brought Abel his clothes and told him everything would be okay. She managed to get her mother to go back upstairs as he made his exit.

A few nights later Lola and her sister Leslie invited him out to go bar hopping. This was when he had to let them know he was only eighteen.

"No problem," said Leslie. "We'll just go to my house. You like screwdrivers?"

"Sounds good to me," he said.

Abel and Leslie hit it off so well that Lola got upset and stormed off, leaving the two of them together. Leslie's husband was serving time at the California Rehabilitation Center for possession of heroin. CRC was a medium security prison for drug addicts and people who were in danger of becoming addicts.

Leslie mixed them a couple of screwdrivers as Lola slammed the door behind her. "To hell with her," said Leslie. "Let's have a good time by ourselves."

Abel took a sip of his drink as he watched Leslie gulp down her glass without taking a breath. After awhile they were feeling no pain. Leslie pulled him into the bedroom and pounced on him like a hungry lioness until they passed out in each other's arms.

Abel woke up early and stole twenty dollars from her purse before he left.

When Lola found out that Abel spent the night with Leslie, she was furious. That didn't stop them from remaining lovers and crime partners, however. They needed each other too badly to let anything like that come between them. They were two sick and lonely people who had found a resting place in their love/hate/passion. He needed Lola with the deepest part of his soul, and would have died in her arms if he could have.

Lola had stolen some checks from her mom and they were going around cashing them at supermarkets and liquor stores. Their goal was to get enough money to buy a large quantity of heroin so they could start dealing. Problem was, every time they made fifty dollars they would go score and get loaded.

They had a favorite place to fix down at the north end of town. They would drive into Haskell Park and park Lola's little Volkswagen in the back parking lot. Sometimes they would get in the back seat and tangle themselves into an erotic frenzy until they exploded into each other with shouts of ecstasy. Most of the time, though, they would just shoot heroin, drink Rainier Ale, smoke cigarettes and nod.

Lola usually did more dope than Abel did, because she had a bigger habit and because "they're my checks and this is my car," she said. Abel didn't care as long as he got loaded and as long as he could be with her. Abel would have let her do anything.

Abel was trying to quit anyway. Well, cut down, at least. If Abel could just get down to a balloon a day he would be okay. He could always come up with the thirty bucks. Now each of their drug habits was over a hundred dollars a day and Abel was getting tired of stealing all the time.

They scored some dark brown dope, the pure stuff, from an ex-con named Sancho. Lola knew him pretty well and arranged the score. They picked up a fifty and raced to their spot in the park. The dope was wrapped in aluminum foil and looked like granulated coffee. Abel smelled it. "Good stuff," Abel smiled.

"Don't just sit there smelling it," Lola sniped. "Get the works out." Abel pulled out an aspirin bottle from the glove compartment that they kept filled with water for cooking up the dope.

Abel grabbed their outfits from under the seat and handed one of them to her. Lola grabbed the cooker and poured in the dope. She filled her syringe with water and squirted it into the brown mixture. Abel tore off four matches and struck them on the cover. Abel held the flame under the spoon until the dope flashed to a quick boil. Lola tossed in the cotton and drew up the dark liquid with her syringe. Abel did likewise.

Abel noticed Lola out of the corner of his eye as she pulled the needle slowly from her arm, suspending it in mid-air for a moment like she was floating in zero gravity space. Abel just finished drawing his dope when Abel noticed she had slumped back in her seat. "Lola," Abel said. "You okay?"

Her head was all the way back, tilted upward with her eyes closed and mouth open. Abel nudged her on the shoulder and she fell against the door. Her face was starting to turn blue. "Hey, wake up!" Abel exclaimed. Abel slapped her across the face and shook her, desperately seeking any sign of life. Abel could tell she had stopped breathing but Abel could still feel a slight pulse. Abel had to act quickly.

What had Abel learned in Boy Scouts? Mouth to mouth. His mind reeled as he jumped out of the car and ran around to the driver's side where Lola was slumped against the door, her angelic face now cast in a deadly shade of pale blue. Abel opened her door and she tumbled to the pavement. He dragged her out of the car. Abel didn't know she was so heavy. Dead weight. Abel dragged her across the asphalt parking lot and turned her over on her back. Abel began mouth to mouth.

She didn't seem to be responding. Abel panicked. "Breathe, Lola," he prayed silently as hope began to slip from his fingers like so many grains of sand. A crowd was beginning to gather around them.

"What's wrong?" Someone asked.

"Too much to drink," Abel lied.

"Somebody call an ambulance!" someone else yelled.

"She'll be okay," Abel insisted.

"She's blue," someone in the crowd gasped.

"Is she dead?" a woman asked.

Abel continued his feeble attempts at resuscitation. Then he did what he had to do. "Does anyone know first aid?" Abel asked.

A young man quickly knelt beside him. "Let me try," he whispered. Abel moved aside and ran back to the car where he had stashed his outfit full of dope. There, while Lola's life hung in the balance, Abel shoved the needle into his vein as the warm arms of paradise embraced him.

Abel tossed the beer and the outfits in a nearby trash can and ran back to Lola's side. He was so loaded now it didn't matter if she was alive or dead. He just knew it was time to get out of here. He could hear the wail of sirens in the background. Lola was coming to. Abel grabbed her by the arm and pulled her to the car as the crowd looked on in amazement. Screech! He burned rubber out of there as a caravan of paramedics, fire trucks and police cars entered the park.

As Lola began to regain consciousness, she whined hoarsely, "What happened to my knees?" Abel glanced over and saw how her knees were bleeding from being scraped across the asphalt.

"Be glad you're alive," Abel shot back as they sped across town, where he dropped her off at her mom's house. He left her in the car and ran down the street.

Their love/hate/passion continued for several months. Abel got a part time job at J.C. Penney's as he and Lola made plans to get an apartment together. Abel was fired for stealing three weeks later.

Lola and Abel fought, cheated, lied, and stole from each other for the next few months. Their relationship hung by a thread. She told him she was moving in with Sancho, her dope connection and Abel refused to accept the truth that she wanted to leave him. She was tired of being with him. She was gone. Abel was alone.

Abel spent the next few days looking for Lola. Her sister Leslie told him she had gone out of town somewhere but wouldn't give him any clues as to where he might find her. Lola was gone and he was all alone.

He wandered downtown, lonely and bewildered in the night. The Eden Valley Fair was in town, carnival lights cast a pale, pastel glow against the sky.

"Hello, brother," the voice was familiar. He turned around to see a black-skinned brother with long dreadlocks standing before him. He recognized him as the one who had confounded him years before with crazy questions, the Prophet.

Abel tried to play it cool. "What's happening, my man," he said.

"The Light is what's happening," the Prophet replied smiling, "and it is within you and all around you."

"I already know all about God," he responded. "I was raised in a Christian church. I've been baptized."

They stood in the center of the carnival. The music and background noises seemed to fade away as the Prophet said, "Don't you realize that you don't need anyone to teach you, but the Light within? That which you have been seeking has been within you and all around you all along."

"Well, yeah, I guess so," he replied, wondering how he had let himself even get so far into a conversation like this. He was beginning to get uncomfortable. "But, hey, I got to go." He started to walk away.

"Wait," there was a deep sense of peace in the Prophet's voice. "Be still and know. Look to the Light within."

He kept walking. What did he mean by the Light within? The words echoed in Abel's mind like thunder. When he glanced back over his shoulder the Prophet was gone.

CHAPTER 9

SLIM

❋

Abel hitchhiked down to Canaan Beach and booked a room at the Clark Hotel on Broadway. The next morning he went down to the Employment Development Department to look for a job. He spotted a card that read, ALARM INSTALLER $5.00 PER HOUR. WILL TRAIN.

He went for an interview with a company called Design Engineering. Larry and Joey were the owners of the company. Two white guys with big ideas about making money. They were working out of Larry's house.

The house was arranged with crystals, pyramids and other assorted occult paraphernalia. "Ever read *Think and Grow Rich*?" Larry asked.

"Whatever the mind can conceive and believe it can achieve," Abel responded.

"You got it," Larry beamed. They looked at each other and smiled. "You smoke weed?" Joey asked. Joey was about forty years old and looked like a holdout from the sixties. He sported an open collar flower shirt, love beads and a goatee.

He hesitated for a moment as he studied their expressions. "Yeah, on occasion," he answered.

"Cool," Larry replied as he reached across the table and picked up a wooden stash box. He opened it and took out a perfectly rolled joint of the best Jamaican herb he had ever smoked.

They sat around for what seemed like hours, smoking weed, listening to Ravi Shankar on the stereo and talking about the nature of thought and reality.

"There is only one universal truth," Larry spouted. "Cause and effect. Everything can be traced back to an original cause, which is ultimately thought itself. Take this table for example," he said. He tapped on it with his index finger for effect. "If they trace it back to its ultimate cause they come to a point at which this table was only a thought in the mind of The Maker."

"Far out," Abel replied. He was stoned into the next dimension but he could still get where Larry was coming from. It all made perfect sense.

"Then even we," he began "were originally just a gleam in the cosmic eye of the universe."

"Precisely."

They gave Abel a pair of white coveralls and sent him on a route with Larry to learn the ropes. The whole idea was to pose as safety inspectors, setting up appointments with middle class homeowners throughout Angel City County. He was assigned to the South Central area because he would fit in with the black neighborhoods. He didn't know it at the time, but he was being used as a front man to rip off his own people.

Once the appointment was set, they would draw a diagram of the home and sit down in the living room with the owner. Using a flip chart, they would show the homeowner how burglaries were on the rise, using excerpts from local newspaper clippings and horrifying anecdotes about brutal beatings, murders and rapes. Having terrified them nearly to death they would go back to the diagram and show them all the ways a burglar could enter their house, take their valuables and attack their children. Then they would describe how theirs was the only system that was able to meet their needs.

"How much?" they would ask. This was the buying signal they were looking for.

"Here's what I'll do," Larry would say as he went in for the kill. "We'll install a local alarm here in the attic," he said, pointing to the center of the diagram. "Then we'll put in your control panel here along with a special intruder alarm at your front and rear doors. Then we'll seal off your doors and windows with magnetic sensors and put in fire alarms in the kitchen, living room and bedrooms."

"How much did you say this was going to cost?" the customer was chomping at the bit.

"That's the best thing about it," Larry grinned. "The whole thing, including fire alarms, panic buttons, and burglar alarm is only thirty nine dollars a month or you can make a cash investment of only eight ninety five."

That was when Larry deftly handed the customer a pen and slid the contract in front of him.

"Just sign here. We'll fill in the rest later," he said as he pointed to the bottom line. "Will that be cash or credit card?"

As they drove away with the signed contract and check in hand, Larry would give Abel a play by play of every moment during the presentation.

"Just get them to agree with you and start nodding their head," he told him. "If you can get the customer to say yes thirteen times in a row, regardless of the question, the next answer will inevitably be yes."

"Wow," Abel's mind exploded with all this new information. They fired up a joint on the way home and talked philosophy and metaphysics.

Within a month, he was their star salesman, making over a thousand dollars a week. He immediately went out, bought used a Pontiac Special, and paid off his back rent at the Clark Hotel. He moved to a new high-rise security building near the ocean. Larry lived in the same building.

It was Larry's birthday and Abel decided to buy him something special. An ounce of good herb would be nice, he thought. He headed back to his old neighborhood to look for a connection. "What's happening, Slim," a dark-skinned brother shouted as he approached. He acted as if they were old friends. Abel didn't recognize him.

"Hey can you give me ride across town?" he asked. "It'll be worth twenty dollars to you."

"I'm looking for some weed," Abel said.

"I'm your man," he replied. "Let's go."

That was the beginning of his association with Ray Ray, the head of a small crew of con artists who shot dope and hung around the beach. The others had names like Roscoe, Graybar, Banjo, and Preacher. They all called Abel Slim because he was tall and lanky.

Ray Ray taught him how to short change. He called it playing the note game.

First, he would buy a pack of cigarettes or a candy bar and hand the clerk a crumbled up ten-dollar bill without looking at it. At the same time, he would engage the clerk in superfluous conversation while another one of them "turned" the manager or blocked the other customers from seeing what was going down.

When the clerk began counting the change, Ray Ray would look surprised and say, "What did I give you?"

"A ten," the clerk would reply.

"Damn, I got all these ones," Ray Ray would say, pulling out a pocket full of bills. "I thought I gave you a one."

"No you gave me a ten."

Ray Ray would take the change and say, "Hey, well, I tell you what. Let me get that ten back for a five and five ones."

The clerk would then take the ten-dollar bill back out of the register and set it on the counter as Ray Ray flashed his bankroll and counted out nine dollars.

"Here. Make sure you count that," Ray Ray would say. The clerk would count the money as Ray Ray picked up the ten-dollar bill.

"Wait a minute," the clerk would inevitably say. "There's only nine here."

Ray Ray would then hand them back their ten dollar bill along with another one dollar bill and say "Well here, just take eleven more with that nine and give me a twenty."

The clerk would count all the money together which would come up to twenty dollars. Not realizing that ten of it was already his, he went back to the register and handed over a twenty.

They headed back to the shooting gallery at Danny's house after Ray Ray had scored about a hundred dollars. In one corner, Abel saw a whore trading favors for a taste of dope. In another corner, he saw a junkie lying on the floor overdosed while others dug through his pockets. Mostly, however, it was just a bunch of dope fiends sitting around nodding, drinking cheap wine and shooting up more dope.

Abel didn't make it back to work the next day. Nor did he ever get Larry his birthday present. After calling in sick for a couple more days of playing the note game, shooting up and nodding, he finally stumbled into work. He looked like he had been washed ashore after a shipwreck. He felt even worse. Larry told him to clean up his act or that would be the end of the job.

Things got worse. He couldn't concentrate on work anymore. He kept on shooting dope. He would sometimes ask a prospective customer if he could use their bathroom and then go in there for a fix. He'd come out nodding, scratching, and asking for a glass of ice water.

Within a month, he decided to quit working. He could play the note game for four hours and come back with two hundred dollars. Why work when he could sit around and nod out in narcotic bliss?

He also learned how to sling hooks. Hooks were fake watches and rings that they could buy in downtown Angel City for less than eight dollars and sell for as much as a hundred dollars each. They even came with a case and whatever price tag you wanted. All he had to do was approach a prospective mark and flash it at him like it was stolen. Like the old saying goes, "You can't cheat an honest man."

"Psst. Hey buddy, c'mere," Abel hawked an old man as he passed. As the old man looked over, Abel opened the case and flashed the watch in front of him.

"Genuine Bulova Quartz," Abel said. If he looked closer, he would see that the inscription read, "Bolivia."

"It's worth two hundred dollars, but I really need the money so I'll let you have it for sixty bucks."

"I'll give you twenty-five," the old man countered.

"Hey, man, you're talking highway robbery. How about forty?"

"Here's thirty. Take it or leave it."

"Alright, here. But don't tell anybody I let you have it that cheap. Since the watch had only cost Abel eight bucks, he would have taken anything over fifteen dollars and still made a decent profit. The fake diamond rings only cost him two or three dollars and he would sell them for twenty bucks or more. On a good day, he could make two hundred dollars. All of that went in his arm.

Abel hadn't paid the rent on his new apartment in two months and the landlady had been leaving nasty notes on his door. It was time to bail. He soon ended up hanging out at the California Hotel again or in the shooting gallery, waiting for somebody needing a ride to go out hustling. He finally ended up writing about five thousand dollars in non-sufficient funds checks to keep his habit going. He kept thinking he would get the money and put it back in his account some day. Even after the account was long closed and he was living on the streets, he still thought that he would somehow take care of it.

He stayed in an abandoned motel for a few weeks while he continued to write bogus checks. He was almost busted a few times when the store computer would indicate a series of outstanding checks, but he always managed to get away before the cops came. He finally got so paranoid that he knew it was time to get out of town. Where was he going to go? He was strung out bad.

Abel stood on the freeway on-ramp contemplating his fate, wondering if he would be better off just jumping into the onrushing traffic. Just as he was about to take that quantum leap, the hands of destiny rescued him in the form of a blue Mustang screeching to a halt in front of him. "Are you crazy?" the woman yelled, motioning him toward the car. "Get in," she said.

She burned rubber as they headed north on the Canaan Beach Freeway.

"Thanks for stopping," he said. He was still in a daze.

"You could have been killed out there. Don't you know it's illegal to hitchhike on the freeway?"

"I know. I was desperate for a ride, and I figured if somebody saw me out there they would feel sorry for me and stop."

"Where you going?" she asked. The woman was an attractive redhead in her mid-twenties.

He wasn't sure. "Los Tecatos," he replied. He didn't know if that's where he really wanted to go but he knew that he could get cheap dope there.

"There's a lot of dope up there," she replied knowingly.

"Yeah there is," he said shooting her a suspicious glance. Is she a dope fiend? He wondered.

"You know I finally found something better than dope," she began.

Oh, no, he thought, *she's going to start talking religion to me.*

She continued. "I don't have to use any more needles and it's a better high than heroin."

He wondered if he would survive if he jumped out of the car.

What she said next made him realize that she wasn't talking about God. "And the best thing about it is that the high lasts over twelve hours and it only costs fifteen dollars a bottle."

"What are you talking about?" he demanded.

"Tussionex," she answered. "T-U-S-S-I-O-N-E-X. It's a cough syrup. Synthetic codeine and let me tell you...talk about smacked back to the max. Yeah."

A familiar grin came over her face and he knew he was in the company of a kindred spirit. Marcie taught him how to call in scripts. She took him to a nearby phone booth and she went to the yellow pages under the heading Physicians. She picked a name and dialed the phone. "Dr. Osgood, please?" she began.

He listened carefully always eager to add a new hustle to his repertoire. "Hi, doctor. This is Marcie Taylor, a friend of Mrs. Smith's. She referred me to you."

Pause.

"She's fine." Marcie looked at him and gave him the okay sign.

She continued. "I've got a bit of an emergency here and I need your help. I'm in town on vacation and I forgot to bring my prescription. I've got chronic bronchitis and my doctor's been prescribing Tussionex. If you could call in a prescription for me here at Rexall Drugs, I would really appreciate it."

"Hey, thank you so much. Marcie Taylor. That's right. The Rexall on Lincoln. God bless you."

She hung up the phone and laughed. "See how easy that was? Now all we have to do is head over to the drugstore and pick it up. And hey, for fifteen dollars this shit will get us both messed up for the rest of the day."

"Cool," he replied.

They stopped at the store and she came out in fifteen minutes with the bag. She opened it as soon as she got in the car and took a big swig out of the bottle, leaving about two ounces at the bottom for him. "Here," she said, handing him the bottle of thick yellow cough syrup. "This will give you a righteous buzz. It takes about a half hour to come on."

He downed it in one big gulp and handed her the empty bottle.

"Now watch this," she said. Marcie opened the car door and smashed the bottle on the ground. She picked up the broken pieces, put them back in the bag, and headed back toward the store. He sat and waited in the car for about a half hour. By the time she came back out, Abel was buzzing. It felt like methadone. His chin was practically in his chest and he had a hard time keeping both eyes open, feeling no pain. He was in heaven.

She got back in the car and showed him a full bottle of the magic elixir. "I told them that the bag broke on the way to the car and they gave me another bottle for free."

"Wow," Abel exclaimed. "This is some good stuff."

Marcie was living in Canaan Beach with her boyfriend Jack, a used car dealer who had done time in federal prison for bank robbery. She invited him to stay the night and told him she would take him up north in the morning. When he told her that his best friend, Randy Gaines' father was a doctor, she offered to take him all the way to Eden Valley.

They headed north the next morning after a breakfast of chorizo and eggs and a bottle of Tussionex. He told her that Randy' father could probably give her a few prescriptions to help her kick the habit. He also lied and told her that he wasn't strung out himself. Fortunately, the Tussionex high lasted until they got to Eden Valley.

He had her pull into the parking lot of Dr. Ed Gaines' office. He went inside first and explained to him that he had a friend who wanted to get off drugs and needed help. He agreed to talk to her. Marcie went in and came out about a half hour later with three prescriptions, one for Darvon-N, a painkiller with a similar chemical makeup to methadone, Lomotil, an anti-diarrhea medicine containing a tincture of opium, and Tussionex for her chronic bronchitis.

Marcie dropped him off in front of his house and thanked him as she headed back to Canaan Beach. "There's a few good pharmacies I can hit on the way down," she said as she blew Abel a kiss goodbye.

CHAPTER 10

BACK IN TOWN

※

To know you
I became a child and lost myself
To dreams and castles in the sand
To be with you
Became my only purpose
As a man
To find you
I sought visions, crystal revelations
Now I understand
To love you
Is to hold you like a butterfly
Not by wings, but with an open hand.

He stood in the driveway for a few moments as he decided whether to go to the door. He remembered that it was the day after Thanksgiving and decided that he could at least ask for a turkey sandwich.

His mom answered the door and he could see the look of suspicion and surprise on her face. She hesitated for a moment before opening the door wider to allow him inside the house. The tension was thick. After all, he had stolen from them. Lied and cheated them. He was a drug addict. An ex-jail bird. Not a favorite topic of conversation.

"Can I just get a sandwich or something?" he asked.

"Of course" his mom replied. "Sit down; I'll make it for you."

Meanwhile, his last dose of Tussionex was wearing off and he was starting to sweat. His nose was running and he knew that if he didn't get a fix within the next hour or so he was going to be real sick.

He did the only thing he could think of at the time. He snuck upstairs and tore a couple of checks out of his mom's checkbook. He would worry about the consequences later.

"Thanks for the sandwich," he said as he left the house and walked down the driveway. He knew he was no longer a part of the family and he didn't really care. He was on his own.

Abel hitchhiked downtown to the shopping center where the Bank of America was located. He wrote out a check to himself for sixty dollars and went inside to cash it.

The teller counted out three twenties.

Abel gave a call to Jay, who picked him up a couple bags of dope. They got loaded in the car. He decided to go back to the bank one more time. He wrote out another check, this time for ninety dollars.

The teller was taking too long. A couple of men in suits approached him and asked him to step outside. The men asked him what he was doing. He told them nothing. They arrested him for suspicion of forgery and shipped him off to the Eden Valley County Jail to await trial. They put Abel in a cell block full of Chicanos. They were all hypes too, so they got along okay, at least for a while. Yogi was there too, so Abel knew everything was cool.

He hung out the first day with Yogi. They swapped war stories and told lies until lights out. Abel was still loaded so he felt pretty good.

"I just realized," Yogi said, "I'll be a dope fiend for the rest of my life."

Abel laughed to keep from crying as he realized this was probably true for him as well. Once a junkie, always a junkie.

A white guy in the cell wanted to start a Bible study but nobody else was interested. They told him to keep it to himself.

Another cellmate was a devil worshipper who bragged about being able to perform real magic by conjuring up evil spirits. When asked to demonstrate his powers, he replied, "The atmosphere here isn't conducive to conjuring up spirits."

"Jail seems like it would be the perfect place to conjure up evil," Abel responded.

"No. Too much repentance," he replied.

There were two six-man cells joined by a common dayroom. The dayroom contained the shower, a couple of metal tables and a television mounted on the wall. There was a video camera outside the dayroom to monitor their every move, supposedly.

With a forgery, Abel figured he would probably get six months in the county jail.

One night Yogi and Abel were playing the dozens, joking back and forth about each other's mothers. A member of Los Vatos Locos prison gang from San Quentin ranted and with racist ravings from the next cell.

"Hey, Yogi, is that a nigger over there talking all that mess?" he yelled.

Abel yelled back, "Yeah, so what?"

Yogi said, "It's okay, we're homeboys."

San Quentin didn't seem to care. "You don't let a nigger talk about your mother, damn it! If you don't kick his butt, we're gonna kick yours. Got it?"

It got real quiet after that. The lights went out. The gates were locked shut. Nobody would be able to go into the dayroom until the next morning at breakfast.

After a restless night, Abel joined the others as they marched down the hallway to the chow hall, hands in pockets, shoulders to the wall. Nobody said anything, but he could tell he was going to have to fight his best friend.

When they got back to the dayroom, the other guys had started putting pressure on Yogi. They told him if he didn't beat Abel down, they were going to beat him down. A skinny youngster named Flaco was the chief instigator.

The fight was on. Abel tried a few of his old karate moves, but years of dope had left him weak and out of shape. Besides, Yogi, who had spent years behind bars lifting weights, was nearly twice his size. Yogi got Abel in a headlock and started pounding him in the face. Abel hit him in the balls and they both went down to the ground. Then the others joined in and started kicking Abel in the face and stomach, leaving him bleeding and unconscious.

The guy who wanted to start the Bible study looked on in fear as the Devil worshipper grabbed Abel and lifted him onto his bunk.

"Leave him alone," the devil worshipper commanded. The others obeyed.

Moments later, a trustee came by to empty their trashcan. A deputy was with him. Abel jumped from his bunk and ran to the cell door.

"I'm not going back in there," he said, his face bloodied and bruised.

The deputy took one look at him and knew what had just happened. "Who did this to you?" the deputy demanded.

Abel just put his head down and remained silent.

"Not talking, huh? Come with me."

Abel followed him to the watch commander's station where a red-faced detective interrogated him for two hours. He refused to tell them what happened, knowing that a snitch jacket would have spelled his certain death sentence. They put him in protective custody until he went to court.

Judge Raincross sentenced Abel to the ninety-day drug rehabilitation program at Carnelian State Hospital.

He went through the program with a positive attitude, trying hard to avoid being sidetracked by the few sexy females who came and went. The program was based on attack therapy. Group encounters. Sensitivity training. Negative feedback. Monads. Dyads. Concept class. "Get real jerks," they yelled.

"Break down those walls!"

"You're not a dope fiend, you're a hope fiend."

"I am a stupid fool who can't listen to good advice."

He graduated from the program and began working as part of the volunteer staff. Graduates of the ninety-day program did volunteer work in various hospital programs in exchange for free room and board, along with training to become drug abuse counselors.

On the day Abel graduated from the Ninety-Day program CJ and Omar, two black guys who had graduated a few weeks earlier, greeted Abel at the gate. They were now working as volunteers. Omar had once been active in the Black Muslims. CJ was a former pimp who liked to tell stories about making his girls work the streets of Chicago in the snow.

Abel got into Omar's car and CJ handed him a joint and opened a bottle of wine. "Welcome back to the world," he said.

Most of them figured that as long as a heroin addict just drank and smoked weed, he was doing all right. That was in 1975, before most of the programs had accepted the 12 step concepts of Alcoholics Anonymous. Instead, they focused on removing defense mechanisms and getting in touch with early childhood traumas, thought to be the root causes of addiction. Behavior modification was used to mold the individual back into an acceptable member of society. It was a strange mixture of Skinnerian Behaviorism with Neo-Freudianism, Gestalt Therapy, and whatever else was fashionable at the time. Transactional Analysis. Games People Play. Primal Therapy. Whatever.

So there he was getting loaded with the rest of the counselors in training, hanging out in staff housing. How were they supposed to teach people to become drug free?

It wasn't long before Omar and Abel headed over to Los Lobos, which was just five miles down the road from Carnelian. Slam. Nodding again. Smacked back to the max. Loaded.

A few days of slamming went by and he was no longer able to function as a counselor. One of the paid staff members, a psychiatric technician, called him in and asked him to give up a urine test. Busted and disgusted.

"Your test results have come back with positive opiate," the director said as Abel hung his head in shame. "What do you want to do?"

She gave him the alternative of leaving the hospital grounds or signing into the long term program known as "The Family." Abel sat stunned for a moment as he contemplated his options. He decided to do the Family thing.

Hard core. They shaved Abel's head and made him wear a dress for the first three weeks. Humiliation was their principle tactic. It was supposed to tear down your false pride and ego, leaving you open to inner change and catharsis. Fascist mind control, like something from the CIA's hidden files, this program turned dope fiends into walking zombies, subject to authority, willing and obedient slaves of an authoritarian system.

The clients had to wear signs and sit in corners like babies while idiots yelled at him for hours on end. Abel slept three hours a night and was awakened in the middle of the night to clean the bathroom with his toothbrush.

Four months of this craziness and Abel was in Phase Two. He was one of Them. Destined to become an Elder. Bill and Ellen Eckart, along with Hymie Maxwell, were the present Elders, or ruling council. Nazi fascists from the Crypto Surf Nazis turned drug counselors. He later discovered they were all strung out at the time they were working at the program.

The last straw for him was when Hymie, a redneck ex-convict with swastika tattoos on his neck, ordered him to wear a sign that read:

"I am a lazy, stinking, no good nigger."

He cursed out Hymie, the rest of the Elders, and all the staff as he threw his sign in their faces and demanded his walking papers. He signed out of the hospital Against Medical Advice and hitchhiked back to Eden Valley.

CHAPTER 11

SOME THINGS NEVER CHANGE

✳

Jay Hanuman was using heavy. He told Abel that Yogi Santana was in the hospital with some kind of some crazy virus. Lola, Abel's old lover and crime partner, was shacking up with another guy.

Abel's parents took him back in grudgingly, making sure he understood the ground rules. No drugs. No drugs. No drugs. "Things are going to be different this time," he promised.

During the next few days, he took a collection of his father's old cameras, watches and jewelry to the local pawnshop. When that money was gone, he stole a couple of their checks and cashed them at their bank. He bought a bottle of Demerol that Randy had stolen from his father's medical bag. Demerol was an injectable solution of synthetic morphine. It came on with a sweet taste and a warm rush of pins and needles. Heaven's bliss. Back in the womb again.

Abel was also out shortchanging almost every day with Jay. When Jay actually worked, he had a good job in the oil fields. That's how he learned to steal copper tubing, which they could sell for quick fix money.

Strung out, Abel was getting tired of this life, but he didn't see any hope of stopping. He couldn't face the pain.

Jay was now married to a young Sunday school teacher. She was jealous of Abel and Jay's friendship. She kept on asking them to buy her some dope so she could get loaded with them. Jay beat the crap out of her in the next room while Abel sat in the living room and watched the baby, nodded and drank ice water.

The next day Abel and Jay went out to score some dope and they got burned by a couple of junkies in Los Tecatos. He hated when that happened. It wasn't worth it, though, to go back out there with guns and shoot a couple of them. They talked about it, though. They figured they could always get some more dope from somebody else. The guys who burned them were the real losers, they figured. They'd just take their money elsewhere.

The money was running out. Abel's game was getting weak. Every clerk in Eden Valley knew his method of operation and refused to sell him anything. The cash registers slammed shut and they picked up the phone whenever he walked in. That's when he knew it was time to move on.

Jay gave Abel a ride out to San Lucio County where he played the note game, shortchanging store clerks throughout the beach towns of Primo, Avon, Shebyl, and Mar Grande.

The cops stopped them coming out of Walter's Donut shop. They were booked into the San Lucio County Jail for conspiracy to commit fraud. They got out the same day on their own recognizance with a promise to appear in court. Yeah, right. Out of there.

Back home. Burned out. Bummed. It was time to quit again. The walls were falling down around him and he needed to get out. He told his father what he was up to. His father wasn't surprised.

***

Abel signed into Genesis Manor, a residential drug program in Cornerstone, based on the 12 steps of Alcoholics Anonymous. Willard Tinsley was the executive director, a flashy businessman and recovering drug addict with over a dozen years of sobriety and experience under his belt.

Billy Rydell was one of the first residents Abel met. Billy was a veteran of programs and prisons, pioneering Narcotics Anonymous in the prisons as he smuggled in ounces of heroin for the Crypto Surf Nazis. Billy had been in Genesis Manor for over six months and was working as a volunteer staff member. In spite of his Nazi affiliations, Abel loved him like a brother. During his stay at Genesis, Billy showed Abel the way of the 12 steps, a spiritual journey into a new dimension of existence.

"You gotta start by admitting that you're powerless over your addiction," Billy said. "That means alcohol, dope, all that crap that's got a hold of you."

Abel shook his head. "Yeah, I know." His hands lay loosely in his lap.

Billy said, "Sounds like you got it that your life is out of control. Otherwise you wouldn't be here."

Abel nodded.

"Then you come to believe that there's a Higher Power that can restore you to sanity. The implication here is that in order to be restored to sanity, you gotta admit you're insane." Billy laughed and slapped his knee.

"That's a tough one. I know I've got some problems, but insane? That's going a little too far. I may be stupid, but I'm not crazy."

Billy lit up a cigarette and blew out a series of smoke rings. He offered one to Abel, who tapped one out of the pack and held it to his lips, cupping in his hand as he lit it.

"In your case, it's the other way around. You may not be stupid, but you are definitely crazy. You know, Einstein said that insanity is doing the same thing over and over and expecting different results."

Abel smiled sheepishly and nodded. "Yeah, I guess I could admit that. It kind of reminds me of that cartoon Wile E. Coyote always chasing that Road

Runner, thinking that the next trick from the Acme Catalog is going to help him catch that bird."

"Yeah, man. You got it, Abel. That's step two."

"I think I get it."

"Now here's where it gets a little tough. At least, for me it did. Step three is where we made a decision to turn our will and our lives over to the care of God – as we understood Him."

Abel took a long drag of his cigarette and closed his eyes as he slowly exhaled. "You know what? I do believe in God. I know that there is something out there somewhere. But I don't know about turning over my will and my life. What if I don't want to go where God takes me?"

"Well, ask yourself this: How do you like where you've taken yourself so far? Great job you've done so far, huh?"

Abel shook his head. "No, I guess not."

"Then you get out a pad of paper and start writing down a list your fears, guilt, and resentments. That's called taking an inventory. You gotta be thorough, though. We're only as sick as our secrets."

"I have a lot of secrets," Abel said.

"Step five is admitting to God, yourself and another human being, the exact nature of your wrongs. That's where you sit down with somebody and read your inventory – all of it."

Abel nodded.

"After that you move straight into steps six and seven: becoming willing to let God remove your character defects and humbly asking Him to do so."

"This sounds like a lot of work." Abel said. "I don't know if I can do all of this."

Billy continued. "Nobody said this was easy. But think about all the work you did trying to stay high all the time. This is easy compared to all that other madness."

Abel sighed. "If I look at it that way, I guess you're right. OK, go on. Tell me about the rest of these steps."

"Step eight is making a list of the people you've harmed, and becoming willing to make amends to them all. If you did a complete step four inventory, then you've already got this list."

Abel said, "Man, that one's impossible. You have no idea how many people I've screwed over in my life. How can I ever face all of them?"

Billy laughed. "You think you were bad? Man, I used to do armed robberies every day. I've killed people in the joint. I've turned women into whores. I've turned guys out in prison. I've done every horrible thing you can imagine and then some. Yeah, nobody said this stuff was easy. I can only say that you just have to start by becoming willing to make amends. You may not ever fix everything you broke, but don't worry about that now. You're still on step three."

Abel took a long drag on his cigarette and blew the smoke out slowly.

"Step nine is where you actually start making amends. But don't get too hung up on how you're gonna right all those wrongs. Just start with the people closest to you, like your family. Sometimes all you can do is just say you're sorry and that you want to make up for any harm you caused them. If they don't want to talk to you, that's not on you. All you can do is make the effort.

Abel wiped the corner of his eye and cleared his throat. He looked away.

"The last three steps, ten, eleven and twelve, are where you start incorporating all the other steps into your daily life. Step ten, is continuing to make amends and admitting when you're wrong. Step eleven, is keeping in contact with your higher power through prayer and meditation. And, as a result of all these steps, you have a spiritual awakening which gives you the power and desire to help others and practice these principles in all your affairs."

For a time Abel began to sense a new hope, a new joy, a new way of living clean and sober one day at a time. It all made perfect sense. There was a loving, forgiving and understanding God and He was available to him, in spite of his ugliness. This God was beyond religion, race, space or time. As he began to tap into this new source of abundant power, he started to experience peace and joy transcending all that he had ever known before.

Then the problems started. Racial problems. Problems with women. Certain people didn't like him. Certain people liked him too much.

Paula was a young, gifted, and beautiful black cocaine addict from South Angel City. Every time their eyes met, there were heart palpitations that seemed as though they were audible to the entire room. There was a shining white light that sparkled in her eyes, and Abel knew it was the presence of the God she didn't believe in. To keep him away from her, the staff assigned him to the Helpline Phones. That meant he had to stay up from eleven p.m. to six a.m. answering Genesis Manor's emergency hotline and listening to people's problems. Here he was, with only two months in the program, giving counseling to horny women who liked to make obscene phone calls in the middle of the night.

The women callers from every background taunted and teased Abel as they described their favorite sexual positions and fantasies. They would inevitably get around to asking him about his sexual fantasies to his delight and embarrassment.

One night he got a call from a still small voice. A young girl named Sarah O'Conner from Cornerstone. Her voice was the embodiment of innocence. She touched his soul with a purity of longing he had never before thought possible. She was an eighteen-year-old virgin who was having problems with her boyfriend. He wanted to have sex. She didn't. She needed somebody to talk to. Abel was that somebody.

She called him every night at midnight and told him everything about herself. He broke the rules and told her everything about himself. Their souls touched in the night. Their hearts danced together until the light of dawn returned them to their respective realities. Their longing for each other remained unexpressed until one night.

Sarah called again. This time something was different. She told him she loved him, that she wanted him to marry her, and that she would take care of him even if he never wanted to work. "I'll take care of you," she said. "I'll get a job and support us both."

She went on to tell him how she had broken up with her boyfriend. That he had been demanding sex and she had refused to give in to his advances. She realized she had been saving herself for just the right man. Abel was that man, she told him.

"You don't even know what I look like," he said, smiling.

"I can feel you," she said. Her voice was soft, like the twilight.

"I can feel you too," he sighed.

"Reach out right now, Abel and hold your arms around me."

He knew what she meant.

There was a pregnant pause. "Hold on a minute," she said suddenly. A long silence followed that let him know she was not on the phone. Something was wrong.

"Sarah. Are you alright?"

No answer.

"Sarah," he repeated. This time more loudly. "Sarah!"

Longer silence.

"Abel, I'm here." She was back on the line. "Something's going on here. I'm alone and I'm afraid. I think somebody's trying to get in." There was a panic in her voice that told him this was real. "Calm down, Sarah," he said. "Tell me what's going on."

"I hear somebody at the window. It's breaking! They're here!"

Dial tone. He didn't have her number. He didn't know her address. Just Sarah O'Conner in Cornerstone. He called all of the O'Conners in the phone book. No luck. His 18-year-old virgin lover was lost in the lonely night.

For three nights, he waited desperately for her call. Just the usual horny housewives, attempted suicides, and manic-depressives looking to for a sympathetic ear. He listened through his tears and nodded in unseen empathy, as his sickened soul grew weary with grief, primal Pain.

He talked with Billy, who listened to his strange story. "Maybe it was all a gag," he said. "You know, some young actress trying out for a part, using you to prove to herself how good she is."

Abel didn't buy it. "Some practical joke," he said.

"Or maybe her boyfriend came over and humped her brains out and now they're living happily ever after," he said.

"Don't joke about it, Billy," Abel was disgusted with his own sensitivity. "You're a sick puppy."

"Well, if you really want my advice, here it is," he said.

Abel looked at him with a mixture of hope and suspicion.

"Turn it over," Billy said.

"What do you mean?" he asked.

"Remember, the third step says, 'Made a decision to turn our will and our lives over to the care of God as we understand Him.' Do you believe in a power greater than yourself?"

"You mean God?" Abel asked.

"A rose by any other name would smell as sweet," he replied. "Trust in God," Billy said. "Let go. Let God do for you what you can't do for yourself."

Abel held his head down for a moment, and then turned to look Billy in the eyes. "I'm not ready," he whispered as a tear began to trace its way to his chin.

"Do you remember the Serenity Prayer?" he asked.

"Yes," he replied.

"Repeat it with me."

They joined hands and prayed in unison.

"God grant me the serenity to accept the things I cannot change. Courage to change the things I can and the wisdom to know the difference. Amen."

The phone rang. Billy and Abel looked at each other hopefully for a moment before Abel stood to answer it. It was her.

Sarah told him that her boyfriend had broken into her house that night and tried to attack her. She said he forced her to take LSD and she flipped out, ending up in the hospital.

She went on to tell him that he didn't hurt her physically but that her chemical and emotional reaction triggered an imbalance in her blood system. "Aplastic anemia," she said. "I'm going to die soon."

He didn't want to accept that, but something deep within him knew that what she was saying was true. He could feel her spirit passing from his grasp as they spoke.

Abel looked up at Billy and sighed. "I need help."

Billy reached over with a tattoo-laced arm and put his hand on Abel's shoulder. "It's gonna be okay, man. I'll help you."

Abel's eyes glistened and he cleared his throat, fighting to hold back the tears of remorse and helplessness. "What do I need to do?"

"Whatever it takes. Whatever it takes." Billy paused for a moment, looking Abel in the eyes, and then bowed his head. "Pray this prayer with me," he said.

Abel bowed his head and repeated after Billy who began, "God grant me the serenity to accept the things I cannot change, courage to change the things I can, and wisdom to know the difference."

Over the next few weeks, Abel came to believe that a power greater than himself could restore him to sanity. He made a decision to turn his life and his will over to a power greater than he was.

Billy asked, "You ready for step four?"

The next day, Abel sat at a desk with a stack of yellow legal tablets and a ten pack of black ballpoint pens, staring blankly into the space between his thoughts. The other residents were downstairs in group therapy. Billy had given Abel special permission to spend two hours a day writing out his moral inventory. He told Abel that he needed time alone, lots of time away from the others. "This is your therapy," he told him. Billy told Abel that he needed to devote at least two hours a day to write in the quiet of my room in order to complete the essential step four in Alcoholics Anonymous – "Made a searching and fearless moral inventory of ourselves..."

This was the third day and Abel was still just staring into space, wondering where he would begin, what I would write, what would anyone reading it think about me?

The sound of approaching footsteps echoed in the hallway outside his room. Abel picked up the pen and placed against the cold yellow sheet, pretending to be deep in literary thought. He couldn't let Billy know the truth - he hadn't written a single word. He was afraid of something, some kind of monster; the creature that he knew was lurking beneath the surface of his consciousness like old Nessie of the Loch, waiting for Abel to trouble the waters. The footsteps pattered past his door and faded into the distance as he sighed in relief.

The momentary relief dissolved as a wave of frustration caught Abel in its ebb. He ran the pen back and forth across the blank page, scribbling lines without meaning, zigzagging from one side to the other randomly, carelessly, dangerously. The zigzags tightened into patterns, rhythms flowed into letters, then words poured out like water, thoughts cascaded onto pages like thousands of stars scattered across as saffron sky as dark, hidden memories sprung forth like geysers from deep artesian aquifers. He thought about Grace.

Once in a lifetime
Beyond all reason and all rhyme
Two lovers from a distant past
Come together once at last

Once in ten thousand thousand years
Casting aside all doubts and fears
A man and woman find such harmony
And finally meet their destiny

And only once as Jupiter aligns with Mars
All of the planets and the stars
Rejoice in long hoped for rebirth
And Heaven falls to meet the earth.

Old realities vanished into space
When first they saw each others' face

And pain dissolved without a trace
As two hearts mingled and embraced.

Once in all eternity
Two lovers find such ecstasy
Ancient friends who finally knew
The One became of what was two.

He finished moral inventory and sat down with Billy to admit the exact nature of his wrongs. He felt a great relief as he confessed all he could remember about his former crimes and lovers.

When Abel came to step nine, making direct amends to those he had harmed, he sat down again with Billy, who had just been hired as a paid counselor for Genesis Manor. "I don't think I can do this one," Abel said. "There's no way I can make up for all the things that I've done to people, all the lying, stealing, cheating."

Billy laughed. "I know you think you were the worst person in the world, but believe me, I've heard your fifth step, and what you did was nothing in comparison to some of the damage I caused in people's lives."

"So how did you do it?"

"To tell you the truth, I'm still working on it. I may not ever be able to make direct amends to every single place I've stolen from or every guy I've shot, beat up, or turned out. I just do what I can a day at a time. You don't have to do it all at once."

"I don't even know where to start," Abel said.

Billy lit up a cigarette and offered one to Abel.

Abel waved his hand and said, "No thanks. I'm trying to quit."

"Good deal." Billy smiled. "I came here to quit drinking and using drugs. That's enough work in itself. One of these days I might get around to kicking tobacco too, but not yet." He took a long drag on his cigarette and blew out a smoke ring. "Back to step nine, though. What I did was start with the one thing I didn't want to deal with. For me, I had to go back to a cop that I beat up while he was trying to arrest me. "I broke his leg and fractured two of his ribs."

"How did you make up for something like that?" Abel asked.

"I went down to the station where he worked, told him I was sorry and asked how I could make up for it." Billy sighed. "I even offered to pay his medical bills or whatever he wanted."

"So what happened?"

"He took me around back and beat the hell out of me. I could barely stand up afterwards."

Abel said, "Like I said before, I don't think I can do this step." He stood up and looked away.

Billy stood up and put his hand on Abel's shoulder. "Let me know when the pain gets too bad."

Abel was kicked out of Genesis Manor the following day for abusing his duties as a phone counselor. They said he would have to wait thirty days before applying to re-enter the program.

He stayed clean and sober for about three more days by attending AA and NA meetings while living on the streets. He couldn't find a place to stay. No job. No money. When he went back to Genesis to get the rest of his clothes, they told him Paula had fallen off a ski lift and suffered a concussion. She had been with another guy at the time. They also told him that he had gotten several calls from a girl who wouldn't leave her name or number. He knew it was Sarah.

Abel hitchhiked to Eden Valley and met up with Jay. Jay lit up a joint and offered him a hit.

An hour later they stole a Volkswagen and headed down to Canaan Beach, where Jay had some good dope connections. Randy turned them on to a bottle of morphine that he had stolen from his dad's medical bag.

Pins and needles rush, warm flush from head to toe, euphoric sensation to the core of his soul. Off to the next connection, they picked up some black tar heroin.

Slam. Boom. Smacked back and nodding into eternity. Heavenly, narcotic bliss. He was in the womb again, home sweet home.

They needed more money before the fix wore off. They stopped by a convenience store where he grabbed a couple of cartons of cigarettes and stuck them under his coat. Busted and disgusted.

They let Jay go. He was white. Besides, he hadn't done anything except steal a car. The cops didn't bother to notice the screwdriver stuck in the ignition.

Angel County Jail. Warrant check. NSF checks came back. Five thousand dollar bail. There was a Bible in his cell. He picked it up and threw it off the second tier to the floor below. Lights out.

The judge sentenced Abel to the diagnostic center at Chino State Prison for a ninety-day observation. They wanted to determine whether he was ready to do hard time. The diagnostic report from Chino recommended Abel for probation with restitution.

CHAPTER 12

211

✳

Back in Eden Valley, Abel told his parents that things would be different this time. He didn't think they believed him, but they let him stay anyway.

He got a job at BUX Records, working in the warehouse as a forklift operator. For three months, he supported his habit by selling stolen records to local record stores for half price. Before long he was so strung out he applied for methadone maintenance at the local county health clinic. They started him at forty milligrams and steadily increased his dose until he got up to sixty. That was enough for him. He would come home after work, drink a couple of beers and nod out in front of the TV.

One night he nodded out while watching a comedy special on HBO. He woke up in the middle of the night and "The Exorcist" was on. He was downstairs alone and the house was pitch black, except for the eerie glow from the television set, as Linda Blair's possessed character glared at him with raging hatred. Terror pierced his heart like an ice pick and he covered his eyes and screamed. Walking backwards toward the TV, he changed the channel to an "I Love Lucy" re-run and nodded out again.

Abel worked the graveyard shift. Stacked cases of records out by the back dumpster. Took them home, stopping at the methadone clinic for his morning dose. Then he would go home and crash out for a few hours. Get up and sell a few albums. Buy some heroin. Fix. Nod out in front of the TV with a quart of Colt 45. Then back to work.

That lifestyle began to burn him out quickly. A security guard caught him trying to pick up a five-foot stack of records from behind the building. They fired him the next day. When he went in to pick up his paycheck, he had a gun in his pocket in case they tried to lock him up.

After losing his job, he got heavier into heroin and alcohol. The methadone wasn't holding back the pain anymore. They wouldn't increase his dose because he was nodding too much. He needed more money.

Abel began casing out a couple of possible robbery sites: the Settle Inn, Lucio Water and Power Company, Howard Johnson's. The .25 automatic he was carrying didn't have a firing pin, but he hadn't really planned on having to pull the trigger. He didn't want to hurt anybody. He just wanted the money.

Abel was driving through Reston Beach one afternoon. He had a couple of outfits under the front seat wrapped in an old bandana that he used to tie off when he shot dope. His .25 automatic was in his jacket pocket. He was loaded on heroin and methadone and he had just finished smoking a joint when a cop threw on his red lights behind him and pulled him over. The cop asked to see Abel's identification. "No problem," he replied as he handed him his driver's license.

"The reason I stopped you is that there have been some burglaries in the area and you resemble one of the suspects," he said.

He had heard that line before.

"I'm not doing anything wrong, officer. I just got lost and I was trying to find my way back to the freeway," he replied.

"What are you doing out this way?" he asked.

"I just came from seeing my girlfriend," he replied.

"What's her name?" he asked suspiciously.

"Jasmine."

"Mind if I search your car?" he asked.

Abel called his bluff. "Not at all. Just tell me if I've done anything wrong first and if I'm under arrest."

"Go ahead and get out of here. The freeway's that way."

"Thanks, officer. Have a nice day." He flashed a peace sign.

The officer nodded, "You too."

135

He drove away slowly and headed out of town.

The next day he pulled up around the corner from the Lucio Water and Power Company. He had used an eyebrow pencil to make himself look like he had long sideburns and a goatee. He wore a red pullover shirt and black sunglasses. He covered his gun with a newspaper. He stuffed a paper bag in his waistband beneath his shirt.

The clerk greeted him with a smile. She was alone. He had gotten a tip from a former employee that the safe contained thousands of dollars in cash. "Excuse me, Miss," he said, stepping up to the counter with the newspaper in his hand. "Can you help me?"

She stepped up to the other side of the counter. The woman was attractive, probably about his age. He wondered what she would have gone out with him under other circumstances.

He showed her the gun beneath the newspaper. "Give me the money. This is a robbery. Move!" he ordered.

She looked at the gun and looked up at him, smiling for a moment as if she thought he was joking. "What is this?" she chuckled nervously.

He pulled back the slide on the top of the barrel to let her know the gun was real. What she didn't know was that it wasn't loaded and wouldn't fire even if it was. "This isn't a joke," he said firmly. "Now open the safe and give me all the money."

She still hesitated.

"Now!" he yelled. Abel pointed the gun to her face then motioned toward the floor safe. "Open it," he said.

She complied by kneeling down on the floor and opening the unlocked floor safe. She reached in and pulled out a moneybag. She put it on the counter nervously. He grabbed it and stuck it in the paper bag beneath his shirt.

"Now lay down on the floor, face down, and count backwards from a hundred," he said as he backed away cautiously, looking over his shoulder. The coast was clear.

He could hear her starting to count as he backed out of the doorway and ran back to his mom's yellow Pinto, which was still idling on the curb. Perfect getaway in broad daylight.

He called up Yogi, who scored a couple bags of good dope for him. He turned him on to a bag for copping and they shot up in a gas station bathroom.

The money was gone by the next day. He had only gotten about three hundred dollars, which wasn't even enough to keep him in drugs for a weekend.

Two nights later, Abel was sitting in his parents' living room, waiting for everybody to go to sleep so he could sneak away and pull another job. This was the easiest way of making money he had tried. He just needed to hit a big enough score so he could buy about a pound of dope, a good car and a nice place. Then all of his troubles would be over.

The Settle Inn on Lindsay Street was his next target. He had already mapped out an escape route through the back roads leading to Lake Eden Estates. He could tell the cops that he had been home all night watching television and he had his mother as a witness. She would never know he had left that day.

Just as Abel was about to sneak away the doorbell rang. It was his mom's friend Nancy Gaines, the mother of his old friend Randy. They had moved out of town and she was here for a brief visit. He greeted her with a kiss and invited her in. His mom hadn't gone to bed yet, so she was still dressed when she came downstairs.

After a bunch of long time no sees, Nancy broke the news that her son Randy had committed suicide. It seems that he had been doing a lot of drugs at the time and was despondent over the loss of a girlfriend. Randy had asphyxiated himself in their garage by leaving the motor running with the door closed.

Abel went in the bathroom and shot up the last of his dope. He had been planning to save some for a wake up but he always seemed to do it all before the night was through. He went to his room and nodded into a deep sleep.

Abel awakened to the familiar panic of withdrawal symptoms: cold sweats, dry heaves, running nose, shaking. He hated this life. He cursed God as he threw on the clothes he had been wearing for the past two weeks. He had plenty of clean clothes to wear in his closet. He just didn't feel like walking across the room. He grabbed his keys to the Pinto and burned rubber to the methadone clinic.

He got there five minutes too late. They had just closed. "Sorry, Abel," the nurse said from behind the glass door as she turned the sign around to read, CLOSED. "You know closing time is nine o'clock. You'll have to come back tomorrow."

"I'm sick," he cried. He was in a panic. He began to double over in pain as his stomach convulsed in dry heaves. He coughed up yellow bile and curled himself into a fetal position, hoping to gain her sympathy. It didn't work. She clicked the door lock, turned and walked away.

"Damn," he cursed as he picked himself up and checked his pockets. He had thirty dollars left, enough for a bag of dope. That would get him well just long enough to make some more money that would buy him enough dope to get him loaded until he needed more. And more. And more.

Night returned. It was time for him to do what he had planned to do. He was hoping to take at least a thousand dollars from the Settle Inn by fear or force. He stuck the .25 auto in his back pocket. Newspaper in hand. Paper bag under his red pullover shirt. Penciled-in goatee and sideburns. Sunglasses.

He left the Pinto running in the back parking lot with the lights out. He entered the office from the back and approached the clerk, who was working all alone. He was about his age, brown hair parted in the middle framing Jay Lennon glasses. He looked like he might be a college student.

"Excuse me, sir," he began, holding the newspaper in front of him and pointing to it. "Can you help me?"

"Sure," he replied as he turned around in his swivel chair. Abel could see that he had been going over some figures on a ten key calculator.

He pulled back the newspaper enough to let the clerk see the barrel of the .25, and then whispered, "This is a robbery. Put all the money in this bag." Abel shoved the paper bag toward the clerk, whose eyes widened in fear. The pupils in the clerk's eyes constrict as the gun barrel stared him in the face.

The clerk turned to the register, opened it, and took out all the money, filling the bag as Abel requested.

"Now lie down on the floor face down, and count backwards from a hundred," Abel ordered as he backed away through the automatic glass doors and vanished into the night.

He headed down the back roads toward his house in Lake Eden, exactly in accordance to his plan. He took off the red shirt and sunglasses and wiped the eyebrow pencil from his face. He put the gun and the shirt in the bag with the money and placed it beneath the passenger seat. He was planning to stash everything as soon as he got home.

Abel was sure that nobody had been following him as he headed up Telegraph Road toward Stanley

Avenue. He could see the row of eucalyptus trees ahead of him as he completed the last mile of his getaway. He entered past the brick gateway to the exclusive residential neighborhood and turned onto Lake Eden Drive. He was almost home.

As he pulled into the long driveway, he noticed a pair of headlights approaching just behind him. Then another light, a red one. Then spot lights. Then a series of doors slamming. Clicks of cocking Glock 9 millimeters and shotguns. Then a bullhorn shouting, "Get out of the car with your hands in the air!"

It was over. His heart sank into a lake of despair as the inevitable unfolded in front of him. He got out of the car slowly with his hands in the air, and saw that patrol cars surrounded his parent's house with at least a dozen Sheriffs deputies pointing guns toward his head.

"Don't move!" ordered the voice over the bullhorn. Abel didn't intend to.

The silhouettes approached him as the red, white, and blue lights continued flashing. He could hear the radio traffic saying, "211 suspect apprehended at residence on Lake Eden Drive."

Click. Click. The handcuffs went around his wrists as they twisted his arms behind his back. "You're under arrest for armed robbery," the officer shouted. "You have the right to remain silent. Anything you say can and will be held against you. You have the right to an attorney. If you cannot afford an attorney, one will be appointed by the court at no cost to you. You have a right to have an attorney present during questioning. Do you understand these rights?"

In his mind, he told them all to go to hell, but what he said was, "Yes, officer," as he hung his head in defeat.

They searched the car and found the money, the gun, and the red pullover shirt. The cops brought the victim to the scene and asked him to identify Abel. "That's not him," he said.

"Are you sure?"

"Yes, I'm sure. That's not the man who robbed me," he insisted.

Then they showed him the bag containing the gun, the money, and the red pullover shirt. "Now try again. Take another good look. Isn't this the man who robbed you at the Settle Inn?"

"Yes. That's him."

The sheriff's deputies took Abel to the substation and booked him for 211 P.C., armed robbery. The law provided indeterminate sentences and the penalty for armed robbery was five years to life in state prison, plus another five years for the allegation of using a gun in the commission of a felony. They also charged him with violation of probation in two counties: Eden County for forgery, Angel City for non-sufficient funds. The next day they charged him with another count of robbery with a gun allegation for the Lucio Water and Power job. They also charged him with conspiracy to commit theft and fraud from the shortchanging beef in San Lucio County. He had a feeling he wouldn't be home for Christmas.

Abel took a plea bargain on the first count of first-degree armed robbery with a gun allegation. The D.A.'s office agreed that if he pled guilty to second-degree robbery, he would be sent to CRC, California Rehabilitation Center in Norco, California. A hospital with gun towers. Prison for dope addicts.

A commitment to CRC meant incarceration for anywhere from four months to two years at a time. There was a seven-year parole period, or "tail," during which violation of any of its conditions meant automatic return to CRC. The program was especially for heroin addicts under the California Institutions Code. The commitment was a civil procedure under which all criminal proceedings were suspended until the program has been successfully completed and the parole board felt you were ready to be released back into society. In order to qualify for CRC, a person had to first be diagnosed as being an addict or "in danger of becoming an addict." All he had to do was show them his needle marks. It was also important not to have a history of violence or history of a violent crime. In his case, the fact that the weapon was inoperable excluded the robbery from the violent crime list. This also kept him from serving an additional five years for the crime of using a firearm during the commission of a felony.

While he was in the county jail going to court, the methadone clinic brought him his daily dose. They tapered it off during the next ninety days, knowing that he was going to be gone for quite awhile.

The charges in Angel City and San Lucio were still pending when he went to court for sentencing in Eden Valley. When they led Abel from the jail to the courthouse across the street, he was chained to an accused murderer on one side and Lola's boyfriend, Sancho, on the other side. He was in for forgery and under the influence of heroin. Lola was in the courtroom waving to him with their new baby in her lap. Abel looked at her and smiled. She pretended not to see him.

The judge was about to pronounce sentence on a young man who had committed burglary.

"I have had a special contempt for burglars," the judge began, "ever since my own house was burglarized last year just before Christmas. The thieves stole all of our Christmas presents."

Abel suddenly remembered that this was one of the houses they had hit during their burglary spree the previous year. He looked at the name on the bench, "Honorable Judge Jeffrey Raincross." That was him alright. If he only knew that he was the one who had ruined his family's Christmas, he'd probably have sentenced him to the gas chamber.

The judge continued, "I hereby sentence you to state prison for a period of five years to life."

The young man reeled as he started to lose his balance. It looked like he was going to faint. The judge continued, "to be suspended as a condition of formal probation. Any further violations will mean you will automatically be sentenced to prison. Understand?"

The young man sighed with relief. "Yes, your honor." The judge was in a good mood. He had just given the young man a suspended sentence.

"In the matter of People versus Abel Adams, is counsel for the defendant present?"

"Yes, your honor." The public defender winked at Abel and motioned for him to stand. The bailiff removed his shackles and led Abel to the center of the courtroom.

After a long lecture about the evils of drug addiction, his potential and last chances, the judge sentenced Abel to CRC. Charges in the other counties were still pending.

He had the privilege of being handcuffed to a guy going to the nut house. Abel didn't ask him what he was in for, and by the looks of him, he didn't want to know.

He arrived at CRC, and was ushered off the bus along with dozens of other addicts. He spent the first several days processing in at a building called the Hotel. This included taking psychological tests, blood tests, urine tests, aptitude tests, and intelligence tests. He discovered that his IQ was 138, just a hair shy of genius. He didn't feel like one.

Abel was assigned to Dorm 23 in unit II, the College Dorm. The dorm consisted of two long rows of bunks with a large common bathroom off one side.

The dayroom and counselor's office were on the front end of the dorm as they came in. The chow hall was down in unit one, also known as The Hotel.

Every morning after breakfast, they were required to assemble in the dayroom as they were read their various work assignments, along with other announcements the staff deemed necessary to their rehabilitation and enlightenment. The University of La Verne provided college classes. They included psychology, philosophy, economics, English, and humanities. He also took classes in typing, accounting, and real estate through Chaffee Community College.

The instructors were helpful in rekindling his intellect beyond the realm of drugs and money. The phrase "once a junkie, always a junkie" began to diminish in its hold over his destiny as he learned to think again.

He read everything he could get his hands on in the field of self-help psychology. He did special projects for extra credit, including programs in transactional analysis and meditation.

His first lesson in economics was TANSTAAFL. "Tonstafel," the instructor pronounced it phonetically. "Anybody know what that means?"

Nobody raised their hand.

"There ain't no such thing as a free lunch," he said, pointing to each letter as he decoded the acronym. He went on to use the example of free pretzels in a beer joint. The more free pretzels you ate, the more beer you drank. A light went on in Abel's head as he began to see things differently.

The Humanities class was based on Alvin Toffler's book *Future Shock*. The premise of the book was that as the world grew smaller and faster-paced through mass communication and transportation, man's psyche was unable to cope with the explosion of new information. According to Toffler, man lost his roots in family, art and religion as he catapulted headlong into the twentieth century's new ways of living in society. The result of future shock was increased stress that led inevitably to the breakdown of the family unit, diseases, alcoholism, drug addiction and crime. The answer to our problems was to return to the basics: family, religion, art. Humanity had to find its roots. We were strangers in a strange land, lost in a vacuous sea of modern technology.

In philosophy class, Abel did a report on the proof of the existence of God. Using the cosmological argument and tracing causes, he deduced a first cause that created everything. He argued that with all of the splendor of the galaxies, the precise harmony of the universe, and the complexity of the human creature; the odds of it all resulting from an accident were astronomical. It would have been like a native walking along the beach and discovering an expensive watch still in perfect condition, and concluding it must have formed there because of the sea breaking along the shore. It would have been like exploding a tree and expecting the pieces to fall into place as a completed set of encyclopedias. He further argued that the law of entropy caused things to fall apart and break down, not come together and become more complex. How could he know that a God whom he had never seen existed? The same way he knew that he had a brain: from all the evidence.

The psychology professor led him through the various forces in psychology, including the Skinnerian model of Behaviorism, Freudian Theory, Jungian Psychology, Erickson's stages of development, and Maslow's theory of self-actualization. Abel learned quickly, and the professor gave him an automatic "A" for the class when he related Maslow's Theory of Self-Actualization to Whitehead's Metaphysics. He postulated that the inner drive toward actualization was the first actual occasion that transcended satisfaction at the levels of basic needs. In other words, our most creative selves were actually enhanced under deprived conditions rather than only when all other drives had been satisfied.

"Brilliant," the professor exclaimed.

English class was a combination of English and American Literature, poetry, and creative writing. He learned to appreciate Shakespeare, Chaucer, Yeats, Shelley, and Coleridge. He especially loved de Quincy's Confessions of an Opium Eater and Coleridge's Kubla Khan. It was here where he also rededicated himself to becoming a writer.

He called his first short story "A Greater Need," a semi-autobiographical account of a junkie who cared more about shooting dope than about the life of his girlfriend whom he watches as she overdoses. As he leaves her to die, he plunges the needle into his arm and injects himself with the same dose she had-just taken so he can join her in eternal bliss. He based the story on his relationship with Lola.

Abel also took classes in counseling, where he learned the techniques of client-centered therapy. The emphasis was on listening and remaining non-judgmental, always maintaining positive regard for the client, and allowing them to work out their own problems.

In his spare time, he pumped iron and hung out with his friend Max, who had gotten busted for Grand Theft Auto. Max and Abel shared a common ambition of making it big in Angel City.

Abel and Max spent long hours discussing the concepts of philosophy, psychology and humanities they were discovering in class. Max told Abel that he didn't buy all this modern philosophy stuff because of an experience he had in jail.

"What kind of experience?" he asked

Max looked around nervously to see if anybody else was listening. "Let's take a walk," he said.

Before the Department of Corrections took over, the property belonging to CRC was once an exclusive resort. As such, it was laid out with large areas of grass with leisurely walkways traveled by life-weary convicts dressed in blue. They exited the weight pile area and walked toward a lonely patch of grass beyond the earshot of eager listeners and skeptics.

"After I got busted," he began, "I was put into solitary confinement." Max took a long drag of his cigarette and looked skyward for a moment, as if in deep thought. "I know I had been doing a lot of drugs for a long time. Heroin, coke, hash, you name it, I was doing it, man. But I swear to you, man, what happened next is the God's honest truth. I swear it."

"Okay, okay," Abel said impatiently, "the suspense is killing me. Get to the point."

"Alright, check it out, man. It was like this, ya dig?" Max tossed his cigarette to the ground and stomped it out. "I started praying, man. I was facing all this time and I just started praying to God. You know? And then all of a sudden I wasn't alone."

"You mean like a cellmate?" he asked.

"Not even close," he said. "It was an angel. I could see him and he talked to me. A real angel, man. Like from right out of heaven."

A strong breeze blew across the yard and Abel felt a chill. Something told him that Max was telling him the truth about a spiritual encounter he had experienced. Max went on to tell Abel how the angel pointed to a Bible and told Max to open it. He opened to the page that began *Whosoever calls on the name of the Lord shall be saved*. "The angel told me to give my life to the Lord and to never turn back. Since then," he concluded, "I've been a new creation."

"Wow," he said. "That's pretty deep."

"Hey, so like it's all about Jesus now. My music and everything I want to dedicate to him," he said.

"But don't you have to give up having fun to be a Christian?" he asked. "I mean, I always thought that dedicating myself to God would mean I had to give up smoking and sex and stuff like that. That's why I just stick with my own philosophy of life. I can't buy into anybody else's religion. Too much control. Not for this kid."

"Well, I haven't got to that point yet myself," Max said. "I still have a whole lot of living to do. But I know that God's working in my life and one day, I'll totally square up and give up everything for him."

"Let's go pump some iron," Abel said.

***

Abel was called back to go to court in San Lucio County to face the pending charge of armed robbery and gun allegation connected to the Lucio Water and Power Company. Before he left, his counselor informed him that if the court convicted him of this additional charge, he would be excluded from CRC and referred to California Department of Corrections.

Arriving in San Lucio jail, Abel was booked and fingerprinted. He knew that if he didn't find a way to beat this case he would be going to prison on this and all of his other charges. When he added up all the charges and their possible sentences it came up to fifteen years to life.

"Where ya from?" asked a longhaired hippie in his cell as the bars slammed behind him.

"I just came up here from CRC, but I'm from Eden Valley," Abel replied, throwing his bedroll down on an empty bunk.

"Hey, I spent a lot of time in Eden Valley. Do you know Leslie Lacey?" he asked.

Of course he did. Abel had been torridly intimate with Leslie's mirror twin, Lola. "Yeah," Abel said. "I used to do that tramp," he laughed. "You know her?"

"She's my girlfriend," the hippie replied.

Gulp! Abel quickly shifted gears and sought to avoid a conflict. He knew the hippie couldn't kick his ass, but no telling what a jealous lover could do to him while he slept. "Hey, wait a minute. You said Leslie," he began sheepishly. "She's a really nice lady. Good people. I really didn't mean what I said a second ago. I was thinking about her sister Lola."

"Oh, Lola," he said. "That whore ain't nothing but a dope fiend whore. She'll sleep with anybody who'll give her a wet cotton."

Abel took a deep breath and decided to get into a whole new conversation. They spent the rest of the day talking about their cases and the various crimes they had committed.

The court made a mistake and went beyond the ten days in which a case must be brought before preliminary hearing. They had to dismiss the charges. He had a feeling this was too good to be true.

It was. They re-filed charges as soon as he got back to his cell. This meant he had to start over again at municipal arraignment, where the District Attorney first reads the charges and asks what kind of plea you want to make.

"Not guilty," Abel replied after the charge of armed robbery was read, describing how he had willfully, unlawfully and feloniously used fear or force to obtain a sum of $320 from the Lucio Water and Power Company.

The public defender, a young curly-haired man, met Abel in the holding cell. "The best deal the D.A. is going to offer is for you to plead guilty to second degree robbery and they'll drop the gun allegation. In case you didn't know, Congress recently passed Senate Bill 42, which abolished indeterminate sentences. In other words, no more five-to-life or two-to-ten year sentences. Instead, the minimum and maximum will be predetermined. For example, in a robbery, the new sentence would be two, three, or four years in prison with the court having the option to give you the lesser or greater sentence in light of mitigating or aggravating circumstances. Therefore, what it comes down to in this case is this: they want you to plead guilty and accept a sentence of three years in prison. The down side is that it could cause you to be excluded from CRC and add another three years to the original charge, which could possibly be run consecutively. Other than that, I say it's a pretty good deal."

No, thanks," he said. "I'll take my chances in a jury trial." Abel stood up and walked away. "

The trial date was set and they began jury selection. He soon discovered that the superior court judge in this case was the Honorable Jeffrey Raincross, the father of his former girlfriend Hillary Raincross.

The trial began on schedule. Abel could tell by the look on the judge's face that he recognized him and that he was dying to convict Abel and give him the maximum sentence allowed by law.

Every time the Public Defender objected, Judge Raincross overruled his objection. Whenever the D.A. objected, the judge said, "Sustained" with a bored look on his face. Even the jury could detect his prejudice. It was obvious to the entire courtroom.

The trial continued for about a week. The key witness made a positive identification, and the D.A. brought in evidence from the robbery to which he had already pled guilty. It looked grim.

Finally, Abel's mother testified to the fact that she remembered him being at home on the day the robbery allegedly occurred. She never knew that he had snuck out of the house that day. She even remembered that he had gone to the drug store to pick up some pictures that day, and that he was only gone for about fifteen minutes. That wasn't long enough for him to have driven all the way to Eden Valley and back, which was at least a forty-five minute round trip.

Then Abel testified and told the jury that he didn't do it. He wasn't there. He stayed home that day watching TV except for a short trip to the drugstore to pick up photos.

The D.A. and public defender concluded with theatrical closing arguments, and the jury went into deliberation. After the first day they were unable to reach a verdict. Abel went back to the cell and spent a sleepless night listening to a guy in the next cell being raped.

The next day Abel walked back into the courtroom a nervous wreck. He waited in a holding cell for the jury to deliberate. He thought about his life. *Who am I? What is my purpose? How did I end up like this? There must be more to life than this.* "God, help me," he prayed. He fell to his knees and prayed a bargain. "If you'll just get me out of this, I promise I'll be good. I'll even read the Bible and go to church." The bailiff interrupted him.

"The jury's ready," the bailiff said as he unlocked the holding cell. He placed the handcuffs around Abel's wrists and led him back into the courtroom. He sat next to his public defender as the jury was ushered back into the jury box. He could feel his heart pounding in his chest. Beads of sweat laced his forehead, and he wiped his brow with cuffed hands. The judge entered the courtroom with the customary "All rise" by the bailiff. "Court is now in session. Honorable Judge Jeffrey Raincross presiding."

The court was buzzing with rumors of the verdict. Guilty? Not guilty? Hung jury? He didn't know what to think. The banging of the judge's gavel interrupted the murmuring. "Order in the court," he barked. "Has the jury reached a verdict?"

The jury foreman stood to his feet. "No we have not, Your Honor. We are hopelessly deadlocked."

The judge was visibly upset. "Does there appear to be a likelihood that a verdict will be reached within the near future?" he queried.

"No, your Honor," the foreman replied, shaking his head.

Judge Raincross sighed loudly, and the jury foreman took his seat. A hush fell upon the courtroom.

The judge scribbled a few notes on the case file, looked at him for a moment, and said, "I have no alternative but to declare a mistrial. This case is hereby dismissed in the interest of justice."

Abel heaved a sigh of relief.

The judge continued. This time he looked directly at him. "Mr. Adams, fortunately for you, the decision regarding your guilt in this matter was not my determination. I understand that you are already serving a sentence at the California Rehabilitation Center and this court has no further jurisdiction in this matter. Therefore, Mr. Adams, you can just go back where you came from."

With that, he banged his gavel, and Abel was free to return to CRC. He thanked God. It was July 7, 1977.

There was one final matter to resolve before he left the San Lucio County Jail. That was the charge of conspiracy to commit theft left over from his short-changing days. The DA offered Abel a deal of pleading to petty theft with credit for time served, which meant the matter would be resolved and he could go back to CRC to finish his program. He took the deal.

He transferred to Angel County Jail, where he had to face violation of probation charges on his bad check case. After convincing the probation office that his problems were all drug related, she recommended the probation be terminated and he be sent to CRC on the original charges.

Abel went back to CRC and returned to the college dorm in time for the second quarter. Max was still there, and he told Abel that he had missed a major riot while he was gone. It seemed that there was some friction between black and white inmates that led to somebody being stabbed to death. The stabbing resulted in an all-out riot. Somebody must have been looking out for him.

Max was working on some new songs and asked for Abel's opinions on them. Abel listened to Max as he performed a solo rendition of three of his latest compositions.

"Right on, bro," Abel said, giving him five. Max was a great composer of melodies, and his lyrics were poetic. Abel told him that he believed he should get those songs published, and that he would be a big success someday. They talked about hooking up after they got out, since they both intended to parole to Angel City.

Abel got out before Max did, paroling to what he thought was a halfway house in West Angel City called Via Sangre, and the place turned out to be a residential drug program with restrictions on leaving during the first four months. After his initial interview, he told the counselor that he would be back in a couple of hours after he picked up the rest of his clothes. After having just spent eighteen months locked up, he told them he needed to take care of some last minute business before he was ready to commit himself to some drug program. He never returned.

He gave a call to Jay, who told Abel he could stay at his house until he got it together. Jay was on the methadone program and still shooting dope. Abel had just received $200 gate money from the parole office that the state gave to newly released parolees to help them get a new start.

Like most people just getting out of prison, the first thing he wanted was some dope. Abel and Jay went in together on a fifty-dollar bag. After being clean for a year and a half, it didn't take much for Abel to get totally wasted. They spent the rest of the day talking about life in prison, dope, women, and philosophy as they nodded and drank ice water.

The following week Abel reported to his parole officer. He told him that he had decided not to go into the residential treatment center and that he was staying with some friends. The officer told him to roll up his sleeves, and after seeing the fresh needle marks ordered him to take a urine test. As soon as Abel handed him back the bottle, he put the handcuffs on him and took him to jail for parole violation. He was on his way back to CRC less than two weeks after he had gotten out. He hadn't even been with a woman yet.

CHAPTER 13

REHABILITATION

❊

Stepping back on the yard at CRC, Max told Abel that he had just missed another riot. This time it was Crypto Surf Nazis against Los Vatos Locos. Abel was glad that he didn't have to choose sides, because he was tight with a number of white boys and Chicanos.

Abel talked his way back into the college dorm, where he enrolled in a course on counseling psychology. He also had a chance to brush up on his typing, and spent his free time reading self-help books and working out. This time it would be different, he convinced himself.

Max had his bags packed. He was paroling to Angel City and was going to live with his cousin Marco, a radio DJ with an apartment on the Westside. Max gave Abel the number to where he was going to be staying and told him to look him up when he got out.

"Don't make the same mistake I made," Abel said as they shook hands. "Don't mess with that smack."

"Hey, man," Max said, shaking his head. "I'm just gonna smoke me a little weed and drink a little bit of the good stuff, some cognac. You know, Remy Martin homeboy."

"Take it light. I'll see you on the streets," Abel said. They pounded fists, snapped their fingers, and pointed at each other like they had pistols.

Max grabbed his bag and headed toward R & R, stopping briefly to turn and say, "You make sure you look me up when you get out, and we'll hook up with some freaks and do the wild thing."

"Works for me," Abel said, smiling sadly. Max turned and exited the dorm with an accordion file under his arm and his bag over his shoulder. Abel went back to doing time again.

Abel stayed in CRC for another four months. When he found out that his urine test had come back negative he tried to appeal the violation, but by the time the appeal was ready to go to the next level, he was already eligible for parole again.

This time he paroled to a halfway house called Back to the Brix. Brix was located in an old converted hospital in Cornerstone. The house contained two programs. Downstairs was for newly released parolees re-entering society; upstairs was a drug rehabilitation center, which used the same attack therapy tactics of Synanon and the Family.

He was assigned to a room downstairs with a roommate named Charles Dubois. Charles had just come out of the California Youth Authority. Youth

Authority, or Y.A., was a reformatory for juvenile delinquents too hard core for camp but too young for prison, known as gladiator school because of the constant gang fighting. Charles was a petty crook who liked to get wasted on angel dust, a mixture of P.C.P. and mint leaves.

Abel was determined to do things differently this time, so he immediately began to look for work. His new parole officer referred him to a counselor at the Employment Development Department, a young black woman who specialized in helping ex-cons get jobs. "I want to get a job working in an office for at least $5.00 per hour," he said.

She laughed and told him not to expect anything better than a job washing dishes for minimum wage, which was $2.25 per hour.

He applied for and got a full time job at Excelsior, a wholesale office supply company, which paid $5.00 per hour. He started as an inventory control clerk and was promoted to order desk within a couple of months. After three months in Back to the Bricks, he had saved up enough money to move out.

A few days before Abel was ready to move, somebody stole a hundred dollars from his pants pocket while he was asleep. He grabbed his roommate Charles by the throat and threatened to kill him if he didn't give him back his money right away. Charles coughed up twenty dollars, which was all he had left after a night of bingeing on craps, cheap wine and angel dust.

Before Abel moved out, he took a copy of a letter that the parole office had given Charles to verify his identity in case he needed to apply for public benefits or obtain a driver's license. He knew that it would come in handy if he wanted to run a few scams under a fake identity. He rented a box at a mail drop in Cornerstone, and applied for a California State Identification Card under Charles' name using the paper from the parole office and the address of the mail drop.

Abel rented an apartment at Ransom Gardens in the Garden District. Max's cousin Marco lived in the same building. Abel turned him on to a joint of Columbian when he saw him in the lobby. Down the hall was the apartment where Max was staying with Cosmo and Lester, a couple of guys who worked as pages at Tinsel Studios. Cosmo and Lester were tired of Max's inability to contribute to the rent and were ready to kick him out. Max was in the process of getting his band together and decided to move in with a hooker on Velvet Boulevard.

Abel's apartment was an unfurnished studio that cost him $190 a month. He bought a couple of pillows and a blanket that served as his only furniture for the first month. He got together with Cosmo, Lester and Max on a regular basis, and they would sit around smoking weed, drinking beer and talking about making money.

For a while, Abel left the heroin alone. All he did was drink beer and smoke weed after a hard day at work. He had it made. He was living the good life.

Later, he discovered that Lester was a heroin user, a man after his own heart. He was involved with a guy named Jo Jo in a series of insurance scams – accident stings. They did some heroin together a few times and talked about different ways to make money. Jo Jo was setting up automobile accidents and cashing in on the insurance. He was in the process of buying a new house, and told him that he also had his eyes on a Rolls Royce. He thought he was exaggerating until he saw him drive up in a Blue Silver Shadow about a month later.

Max later hooked up with a beautiful model and actress named Lee. Lee was a gorgeous Christian girl who was always praising the Lord and trying to convert everyone in sight. Abel resisted her evangelization attempts the best he could, but he did allow her to pray for him and bless his apartment.

One night Abel took the bus to Cornerstone to pick up his mail. A box of checks had arrived from the bank. He had ordered them using the new California ID card with the assumed name of his former roommate from the halfway house, Charles Dubois. After picking up the checks, he ran across the street to the bus stop and tripped in a pothole. He felt an excruciating pain in the side of his foot, which had come down hard on the broken asphalt. He knew his ankle was sprained because he couldn't move it, and it began to swell up right away.

In spite of his pain, Abel made it back home on the bus and fired up a joint. He made an ice pack and wrapped it around the ankle to avoid the swelling. About an hour later, the doorbell rang. It was Max. Abel invited him in and told him about his little accident. He laughed when he saw his swollen ankle.

Max had brought a half gallon of Chablis Blanc with him, and Abel could tell he was already pretty drunk. He started giving him a sob story about how Lee was treating him. Abel asked Max to run across the street and bring him a bottle of vitamin C and some aspirins.

Max came back in a few minutes with the aspirins and vitamin C, and they spent the rest of the night drinking wine, smoking weed, and talking about their problems with women.

Abel had just started seeing Rosie, a gorgeous young welfare mother with two kids. She had invited him to spend the night with her a few times, and he could tell she was already getting serious. What she wanted was a man to be a daddy to her two sons, but Abel wasn't sure he was ready for that yet.

The next morning, Max helped Abel hop down to the neighborhood supermarket. He saw a place where they sold indoor plants. The floor was wet where they had been watering the plants. He slipped and fell. Max was his witness. The manager called the ambulance after taking pictures of the scene and asking him a few questions.

"What happened?" he asked.

"He was just walking along here and he slipped and hurt his ankle," he said.

"Were there any injuries to your foot or ankle before you slipped and fell here today?" he asked.

"No, I was fine until just now," he lied.

Max broke out laughing, and Abel shot him a warning glance. The ambulance arrived and took Abel to an orthopedic doctor who took x-rays, determined there was a chipped bone in his foot, and fitted him with a cast and a pair of crutches.

Two months later, Abel had a check from the insurance company for $2500. By this time, he had already gone on a spending spree with the checks he had obtained under an assumed name. His apartment was furnished and he had a brand new wardrobe.

Meanwhile, Max's roommate Cosmo was telling Abel about his plans to make it big in Angel City as a screenwriter. Abel was impressed by his knowledge of the industry and by his ambition to be a writer. He was especially impressed when Cosmo told him that one good screenplay could sell for over a hundred thousand dollars or more. He told Abel that he knew certain writer/producers who were earning as much as ten million dollars a year.

Abel got tired of his job at Excelsior after about a year, and he decided to branch out in a different direction. He was just about ready to go into business with Jo Jo and Lester on a staged accident when he heard the news from Cosmo. Cosmo told him that the car Lester was driving exploded when it was rear ended by the rental car Jo Jo had paid somebody to drive. Lester died at the scene, burned to death. Jo Jo was later arrested on federal racketeering charges and sent to prison.

CHAPTER 14

MEPHISTO'S PARADISE

✳

Vincent Sinclair was a handsome man with a distinct European accent, in his mid-forties with a close-cropped beard and a receding hairline. He was the president of a newly formed corporation called Mephisto's Paradise, Inc. Sinclair told Abel they were in the final stages of creating a new line of gold pendants called "Paradiso." Paradiso was the creation of award winning jeweler to the stars, Jorge D'Angelo. Paradiso consisted mostly of ancient symbols that were said to have magic qualities. When gazed upon, they were supposed to render the viewer hypnotized.

It sounded like an excellent idea. Abel told Sinclair about his background in sales and marketing, and Sinclair invited him to his home in Sunset Coast.

Abel arrived at Sinclair's home, nestled around the cliffs overlooking the shoreline. The house was a two-story redwood with a large bar in the middle of the living room, a den and large master bedroom. Abel noticed a bag of Sinsemilla on the table, and he knew that this would be an interesting business meeting.

Abel was dressed in a navy pinstriped suit and red power tie. Sinclair wore Guess jeans and an open-collared Armani shirt. He offered Abel a glass of wine, which he graciously accepted. Sinclair fired up a joint, "Do you indulge?" he asked.

"Absolutely!" Abel replied eagerly. Sinclair handed Abel another joint along with a lighter and motioned for him to fire it up.

Their conversation began cautiously. First, they talked about the house and Sinclair showed Abel around. Abel commented on the quality of the marijuana they were smoking and Sinclair said that he always kept a good supply on hand. About half an hour later, they were interrupted by the arrival of one of the most strikingly beautiful women Abel had ever seen.

Sinclair introduced her as Elle, his personal assistant. She looked to be in her early thirties, long jet-black hair with a streak of grey in front that offset her pale white skin with a look of haunting seduction. The moment she entered the room, Abel struggled to keep his eyes off her.

Sinclair commanded Elle to fix them a tray, as he motioned for Abel to join him in the den. Elle returned within half an hour with a snack tray overflowing with various cheeses, crackers, and more wine and weed.

Abel became a regular guest at Sinclair's house. After his second visit, Sinclair brought out the cocaine. They spent hours in deep conversations about metaphysics and philosophy. Sinclair was really into astrology and told Abel that he was getting ready to enter the time of Saturn's Return. He said that Saturn returned to the same points in relation to the earth every twenty-eight years and that at age twenty-eight his life would begin a radical change.

Sinclair was also a vegetarian and he taught Abel that all of the great socialists of history such as Hitler and Stalin were vegetarians. "What about Jesus?" Abel asked.

"Look how he ended up," Sinclair replied, giving a long sinister looking smile and snorting a line of cocaine.

"According to Sigmund Freud," Sinclair said, "Cocaine would cure all the world's ills."

"I don't know about that," Abel said, "but I like the way it makes me think. It expands my mind toward its ultimate potential. I can see more clearly how the universe works."

Sinclair thought what Abel was saying was very interesting and ordered Elle to get a tape recorder so that what Abel was saying could be saved for posterity.

The conversations got deeper. Abel drove Sinclair around town in Sinclair's vintage Rolls Royce as they talked about the nature of reality. Sinclair especially liked talking about the relationship between men and women.

"You know the only real men in the world today are pimps," he said.

"I know," Abel replied. "It's all about the game."

"Exactly!" Sinclair always started to get excited when he showed some insight into the meaning of life and its philosophies. "You know old J.C. was a pimp don't you?" he asked.

"J.C.? Who's that?" Abel queried, not wanting to look too stupid. "You mean Jesus Christ?" he asked.

"Don't say that name," he cursed. "Just listen damn it. Sometimes it's better to just listen."

Something wasn't right about what he was saying, but he went along with it for awhile.

"You know the snake in the Garden of Eden was the first real man," Sinclair continued. "Adam was nothing but a trick. The snake took his woman and made him out to be a fool.

That's why they still have three kinds of people today — pimps, hos, and tricks. The only real man is a pimp."

Sinclair went on to expand upon his worldview that included an idolization of fascist dictators throughout history, astrology, numerology, sorcery and the occult culminating in a plan by a group he referred to as "The Masters" who were supposed to take over the world according to an ancient plan. Sinclair told Abel that he was a key part of this plan and that Mephisto's Paradise, Inc. was just a front. He gave Abel a copy of *Initiation* by Alice Bailey and told him to study it. "This is what they're really all about," he said smiling with his all too familiar grin.

Abel soon realized that what he was involved with went beyond politics, business, and even religion. There was an evil force, of which Sinclair and his cohorts were just a part. It was all about control. Control of money, control of women, mind control, drugs, the occult, Satanism and sorcery.

"How do I get to the next level of consciousness?" he asked.

"You have to die first," Sinclair replied.

The words echoed in Abel's head. He didn't know if it was just the cocaine that started making him paranoid, or if it was the fact that they were after him that made him want to do more cocaine. He needed to stay sharp, he needed to stay aware, and he needed more cocaine.

The long nights of philosophical discussions turned into drug-frenzied orgies as dozens of gorgeous women paraded in and out of Sinclair's house every night. Abel got so amped up that he could see electricity in the air. He called it Electric Avenue, and it sounded like running water. Sometimes he would just get up and run out of the house, wide-eyed with terror.

Abel ended up losing his apartment and asked Cosmo to give him a place to crash for a couple of weeks. Cosmo was more than gracious even though he was barely making it himself. Cosmo consented and they stayed up late at night smoking marijuana and talking about religion. After telling him about his fears regarding Sinclair and Paradiso, Cosmo recommended that he start reading the Bible.

"Check out the Gospel according to John," Cosmo said. "And if you really want to blow your mind, read the Book of the Revelation."

Abel took Cosmo's advice and stayed home the next couple of days reading the Bible and smoking marijuana. After reading the Revelation, he ended up getting more confused about his relationship with Vincent Sinclair.

"Was this the Antichrist?" he wondered as he read the part about the mark of the beast — 666.

Abel finally gathered the courage to go back over to Sinclair's house. As always, there was plenty of wine, weed and cocaine. Abel was unable to resist and within one hour, he was stoned again, listening to Sinclair's ramblings about the coming kingdom of darkness. Abel could hear the thundering hooves as an image of a pale horse galloped through his head. The rider was Death. "You have to die first," Sinclair repeated.

Darkness fell upon them. Elle and Abel stood silent as Sinclair continued what seemed like a satanic sermon on the mount. As Abel gazed into Sinclair's steely blue eyes, they seemed to stare back at him from a place far away from this earth, a place of evil. Sinclair's face began to change shape as he continued talking of the powers and principalities in high places and the Master's Plan. For a moment, Abel didn't know whether he should kneel down at Sinclair's feet or run screaming into the night in stark terror. He found he could do neither. He was paralyzed, as he stood and watched Sinclair's face as it changed into the image of something very demonic. He was staring face to face with the personification of evil, and he didn't know what to do.

Abel gulped down the rest of the red wine in his glass and came back down to earth. He just stood there motionless for a while. Sinclair announced that he was tired and was going to get ready for bed. As Sinclair turned and walked away, Elle and Abel looked at each other in amazement.

"Did you see that?" she said. Her eyes glistened with a bit of glee, or was it terror?

"See what?" Abel asked, trying to play it off. Abel wanted to believe that he had just been hallucinating.

"His face," she said. "It was like looking at your grandfather."

Abel wasn't sure exactly what she meant, and he wasn't sure he really wanted to know. All he knew was that it was time for him to go.

Abel jumped up and ran outside to his car, screeching out of the driveway and down the long hill toward the highway.

CHAPTER 15

FATHER TRUTH

✳

Within me
Is the seed of magnificence.
Unlimited perfection
As natural as the earth,
As powerful as the sun,
As personal as my own heartbeat.
It is the essence of love,
The source of life,
Purpose fulfilled

Cosmo was tired of Abel taking up space and told him so. Abel packed up his books and clothes and went to see his parole agent. He told his parole agent the truth -- that he was down and out with no job, no money, and no place to stay. His parole agent set Abel up in a single-room occupancy hotel down in Cornerstone. At least now, he had a place to lay his head and store his stuff. He took the last few dollars that he had and went to the racetrack.

After losing every cent he had, Abel drove toward the beach on the Soto Freeway. As he headed toward Reston Beach, he saw a familiar green BMW pull up next to him. It was Elle. She smiled and waved, then pointed toward the Reston Boulevard off-ramp with a question mark look in her face as if to ask if he was going back to Sinclair's house. She got off the off-ramp and he kept on going straight. It was the last time he saw her.

Abel parked his car on a side street in Reston Beach. It was still full of clothes that he hadn't finished unloading into his hotel room. He was totally broke, hungry and almost out of gas. He had to come up with a hustle somehow. His mind was still in a daze from weeks of sleepless nights, high on cocaine, marijuana and alcohol.

Abel started walking along the Boardwalk as he contemplated his situation and his fate. What was he going to do? Who was he? Where was he going? He was lost in the wilderness of confusion, wandering aimlessly in the desert of his mind, a stranger in a strange land.

A stranger approached. Abel could see the young man coming toward him. *Was this some panhandler imagining himself to be in worse financial conditions than he was? Was it some gay blade looking for a fancy? Worse, another devil worshipper seeking to use him as a blood sacrifice?*

Too late to change directions. The stranger was standing in front of him. He extended his hand in an offer of friendship and said, "Hi, my name is Ishmael, how are you doing today?"

Abel eyed the stranger suspiciously, as he reluctantly responded to his outstretched hand. They shook and Abel responded with a mumble, "Okay, I guess, what's up?"

"I'm out here talking to people about a new way of solving problems in the community and I'd like to get your input," he said, "Here's a card. A lot of us get together every evening for dinner and we discuss things like religion, philosophy, science and politics."

"Hmmmm," Abel grumbled, "I'm real busy tonight so I don't think I can make it," he lied. He didn't have anywhere to go. He wasn't even sure where he was going to spend the rest of the day.

"Are you hungry?" the man asked.

Abel hesitated for a moment, looked away as if to find a route of escape, then hung his head down, "Yeah," he replied.

The house was just a couple of blocks from where they stood on the Boardwalk. The sun was beginning to set on the ocean behind them casting a purple haze over the beach.

Ishmael opened the door and gestured for him to follow him inside. Abel could smell the aroma of soup coming from the kitchen, and he noticed a stringy-haired blonde girl in there cooking. There were a couple of other women cleaning and dusting throughout the other rooms in the house. They beamed wide-eyed smiles as Ishmael introduced him to them all.

"Welcome," said the girl in the kitchen. "Would you like some soup?"

"Sure would," he said.

Abel and Ishmael sat in the living room as the girl brought them out a couple of bowls of thick vegetarian soup and a pitcher of iced tea with lemon.

After a few minutes of small talk, Ishmael started talking about values and society from a historical perspective. It sounded interesting and Abel commented that at present the only things he valued were money and power. Ishmael looked shocked by his response but continued to elaborate on his description of modern society, its ills, and the causes of their current predicament.

"The cause of crimes is selfishness, or misdirected love," Ishmael announced.

Abel thought that Ishmael was starting to make sense. He wondered if he could incorporate the techniques of this organization into his own system and start a motivational consulting firm of his own. He rang up dollar signs in his head as he imagined being the head of a large network of educational seminars. He pictured himself becoming the head of his own new religion, a new age guru.

After dinner, Ishmael presented an outline of world history on a blackboard, beginning with the creation of the universe and culminating with the second coming of the Messiah and the ushering in of the Kingdom of Heaven on earth. Ishmael said that this new Messiah was now here on earth living among them and his name was Father Truth.

Father Truth was born in El Salvador to a family of converted Lutherans. At the age of 12, he claimed to have received a vision of Jesus Christ while praying on a Salvadoran hillside. The apparition appeared to him, telling the young boy that the mission of Jesus had failed and that God needed another Messiah to win victory over Satan and win a final victory for the Kingdom of Truth.

After studying various disciplines of science and religion, Truth started the Universal Association for the Truth of Absolute Reality, also known as the Truth Church, or Truthies. The Truth Church was based on the progressive revelation of God to Father Truth, whom church members affectionately referred to as Papi. Father Truth, they were taught, was the personification of God on earth, not only equal to God, but actually greater than God.

To complete his indoctrination, Papi sent Abel to a weekend retreat at Camp Revelation in the San Rialto Hills. The weekend turned into a weeklong training session where he received training in the Divine Truth, the Bible of the Truth Church written by Father Truth.

According to the Divine Truth, Jesus Christ failed in his mission to create the Kingdom of Truth on earth by ending up on the cross instead of on the Throne of

David. Truth taught that the original Eden was located in El Salvador and it was from there that a new Messiah would come to rule and reign after Satan was finally defeated.

As Abel's indoctrination continued, they transferred him to a camp in northern California called Stoneville. Every day consisted of scores of new recruits spending 20 hours a day in repetitive lectures, song worship services, small discussion groups, and manual labor on the farm. They ate light vegetarian meals and slept about four hours a day.

Abel emerged from this month-long series of indoctrination totally convinced that God chose Father Truth and his followers to win the world back from Satan. Their mission would obviously require hardball tactics like those used by elite units of the CIA and National Security Agency. They would need large sums of capital, massive stockpiles of weapons, and an unlimited source of fresh labor. Toward this end, Father Truth owned scores of financial interests including armament factories and manufacturing plants in Mexico, real estate holdings in South America, and distribution companies in the United States.

Papi also owned a vast publishing empire, an artwork distributor, a soft drink bottling company, and a large fishing fleet based in Babylonia.

Young converts like Abel who sold flowers, jewelry, and cheap artwork door to door and on street corners raised most of the money, tax-free. In addition to fundraising, the church was heavily involved in recruiting new members. At the time Abel was involved, the church claimed to have 80,000 members in the U.S. and over one million members worldwide. Most of the recruiting took the form of street witnessing, which involved going into various areas and inviting people to dinner. They concentrated on tourist areas and places where students congregated.

After the training in Stoneville, he stayed for a while in a different mansion the church owned in Babylonia. The leaders took them out in the mornings in vans and dropped them off in small groups near Seaman's Pier or at U.C. Babylonia. The church also had a number of front organizations for witnessing or bringing the messages of the Divine Truth to the masses. One of these was the People's Community Project in Babylonia, designed to attract foreign tourists and young disillusioned intellectuals. Potential converts would not hear any references to Father Truth until they arrived for training in the farm at Stoneville.

Another front organization, the Student Association for the Research of Truth or SART, was a campus-based political action group designed to convert young college students through its strong socialist views and promotion of strong environmental values.

The church also sponsored an annual World Conference on the Truth of Science and Spirituality with the intention of converting world-renowned scientists and religious leaders. The church also owned the Truth Theological Seminary in Shakely, created to train future leaders in the Truth Church.

Father Truth was married to his fourth wife, Milagros, and was the father of seven children. The family was the center of Truth's plan for world restoration and every several years he would gather together thousands of his followers for a mass wedding ceremony. Truth would handpick the spouse of each member and bind the couples in a ceremony that included drinking wine mixed with Papi's own blood. This was supposed to cleanse the couple of the original sin, who in turn would give birth to sinless children. Their sinless children would then become the founders of an ideal society free from crime and disease.

After returning to Reston Beach where he spent about one month fundraising, witnessing, and teaching Papi selected Abel to go to Phoenix, Arizona for a special advanced training session. The session lasted for three weeks and concluded with the proposition that Father Truth was not only God in the flesh come to finish what Jesus started, but was literally greater than God, because he was now the ruler of both worlds: Heaven and Earth.

After the training, the leaders assigned him to a Mobile Moneymaking Team, or MMT. Their base was in Moriah, Washington and they were responsible for covering Washington, Oregon, northern California, and the State of Wilderness.

The MMT was a military-like operation headed by an El Salvadoran commander named Mr. Guerra. A captain was assigned to each state. The fundraisers would ride to various areas in big vans. After arriving at their predetermined area, they would fan out in military precision with boxes of products under their arms. Products were usually flowers, candy, cookies, jewelry, or cheap artwork. Most of their products had at least a one-thousand percent mark-up. For example, long-stemmed roses would cost them about $0.20 each wholesale. They sold them for $2 to $3 each.

The MMT members sold metal etchings and laser art prints, which cost $0.50 to $1, for as much as $25 each through their True Products Division. Sometimes they would even run across members of other groups like Scientology and Hare Krishna, who would be out fundraising with the same products. They would then have to work twice as hard to get to all he most lucrative areas before they did.

They lived on the road and slept in the van, subsisting on tuna fish and peanut butter and jelly sandwiches. They washed themselves in gas station bathrooms and wore the same clothes for days at a time. They were encouraged to keep their hair short for ease of care.

Every morning started with a devotion to Papi. They sang an El Salvadoran song together, and then bowed three times before the picture of Papi and his wife, Milagros. They would pull over to a restaurant or gas station where they could clean up and their captain would give them each a sandwich and a cup of water to start their day.

Before getting out of the van, they would check to make sure they had enough products to meet their goal for the day.

Abel usually averaged about $300 a day. Anyone who came back with less than $100 was usually humiliated and forced to go back out until they made their goal. Sometimes, they worked until ten o'clock at night. At the end of the day, they had to share about their day and how much money they had brought into the Kingdom of Truth.

After about a year of working in Washington, Oregon, and northern California, they gave Abel a plane ticket to Wilderness where he joined the MMT up there. Wilderness MMT was an elite group of fundraisers who had proven their ability to work long, hard hours without much supervision.

Their base was in Goshen, where bustling fishing and oil industries brought in a big money flow. The inhabitants of Goshen were a rugged, outgoing bunch, most of whom were big spenders and heavy drinkers who liked to stay out late and have a good time. The sun didn't set until two o'clock in the morning, and the bars stayed open until 4 am.

Late at night, the MMT would blitz the downtown areas by hitting the bars so fast the owners never knew they were there. Bars were great places to sell flowers and jewelry and the Truthies used to deny any religious affiliation to keep the customers from feeling guilty about being in a strip club. Abel used to hang out in bars and show off a few pieces of cubic zirconium or a gold-filled chain. He would average about $1,000 per day. He sent the money back to Goshen headquarters by bank wire on a daily basis.

On several occasions, Abel was sent on special assignments to small Wilderness villages along the Yarmak River or down at the end of the Arhatian chain. The natives were friendly for the most part, although sometimes they expressed hostility toward the white colonialists who had raped their land and women. Abel was glad to be a non-white at the time.

The Wilderness natives he met were generally of three distinct types: Sebastos, Endorans, and Arhats. The Sebastos were a peaceful, friendly people with bright smiles whose primary occupation was fishing and whaling. Once a native couple, after buying about $100 in gold jewelry from him, offered him a special treat — whale blubber. It was white and looked like big chunks of candy. He put a piece in his mouth and started chewing and chewing and chewing. His jaw started aching. The stuff didn't dissolve like he had hoped. Instead, it just remained a big glob of fishy-tasting wax. "Like it?" they asked.

"Good," he mumbled. His mouth was still full. He didn't want to offend them. "Oh, well here, have some more," the Sebasto responded as he chopped off another big chunk and wrapped it in plastic for him.

He stuck it in his backpack and promised to eat it later. As soon as he was out of sight, he threw it in the trash.

The Arhats lived along the Arhatian chain that stretched from Dunham to Dead Harbor. They were a rustic bunch with a lot of resemblance to the early nomadic settlers who brought their animist religion to Wilderness during the previous century.

The Endorans were a rugged breed of natives that lived along the mighty Yarmak River, between Fremont and Marion. They were the most noticeably hostile to the white race. Once when Abel was in a bar in Fremont, he came across a native who had done his share of drinking. When he approached him, he began ranting and raving about how the white man had ruined his life with their lies and treachery. He blamed the white race for his drinking and for his poverty.

Abel thought to himself the words, God loves you.

The native's next words surprised Abel. Suddenly the man's expression softened and a single tear began to trace its way along the ridge of his ruddy cheek. "God loves me," he said and then he began to sob.

Abel's time alone in the Wilderness bush country was exciting. Everyday brought a new adventure. He practiced what they called "Heavenly Deception," which was another way to say that he lied about being a Truthie.

"You with that Salvadoran Nazi, Father Truth?" the owner of a bar once asked.

"No way dude," Abel lied, "I work for myself and I'm saving money for college."

"Okay, well let's see what ya got," he said. Abel ended up selling him a turquoise eagle on a silver chain for $50.

During his various missions to the Wilderness bush country, Abel broke a lot of rules in order to fit in with the locals. He smoked Thai sticks in Tamarack, drank beer in Belmont, and slept with a beautiful native girl in Nantioch.

Once as Abel was running along the beach to the next village, he saw an eagle soaring just 20 feet above him. As Abel watched the bird soar effortlessly with outstretched wings, he stopped and revered God's creation. Tears ran down his cheeks and he sobbed uncontrollably for a long time.

Another time, he sat along the Yarmak River as the rain subsided and the sun beamed forth in a surrealistic sunset. Three rainbows appeared at the same time above the river.

After his last mission in the bush, he returned to Goshen and was assigned to sell a collection of mass produced oil paintings. The pine frames were made in Mexico and the canvases were painted in an assembly line in China. The pictures cost them $10 to $25 apiece, and he was selling them for an average of $300 each.

Abel was starting to get burned out. They sent him out with a partner, Hannah, a tall, long-legged and lovely brunette from Sweden with azure eyes like the Wilderness sky. He wanted so badly to take her away with him or just to hold her in his arms one time. But the guilt instilled over the last year and a half of religious indoctrination into one of the world's most powerful mind controlling cults had made him cringe at the thought of ever dragging his innocent sister with him into hell.

As Abel fundraised along a downtown Goshen street, he came across a used bookstore. He entered and began to browse among the shelves. He was looking for a way out, perhaps he'd find an answer here, he thought. He came to the section marked, "Self-Help/Psychology." It was next to the section on "Occult/Metaphysics." Somewhere between the two sections, he found a book called Reawakening and Rebirth by Oscar Kilgore and Raylene Divine.

The book described a system of personal transformation and growth, which resulted from getting in touch with and letting go of birth trauma. That was it, he thought. This was what he needed. He skimmed through the book some more and decided it was something that he needed.

He kept the book with him and read it over the next two days as his fundraising results plummeted to zero.

"What's wrong Abel?" asked his partner Hannah. "You were doing so well before, but now you seem like you're just not motivated anymore."

"I need a reawakening," he replied, knowing she wouldn't understand what he meant. He looked at her with longing and decided it was best if he continued to keep his feelings to himself.

The next day, he looked through a phone book in the yellow pages trying to find a listing under the title "Reawakening." No luck. He checked under "Transformation." No luck. Finally, he checked under "Health Consultants" and found a woman named Darcy who did reawakening. He called her and arranged to come right in. He met her in a holistic health center run by Sikhs, a religious group which somehow combined the teachings of Yoga and Sufism. Darcy was a seductive looking brunette with an upturned nose that reminded him of a kitten. She wore a mink jacket and a Cartier diamond watch. As she led him downstairs to a private room, he felt like he was about to have an interlude with an expensive masseuse, the kind that worked at the massage parlors along the Strip. One thing he knew for sure was that he was about the experience something that would deeply affect the rest of his life.

After directing him to take off his coat and boots and loosen his clothing, Darcy pointed to a mat on the floor and asked him to lie on his back. He followed her directions as she guided him through a process of circular breathing, which he was told would allow him to get in touch with his birth trauma in order to release him from its affects in his life.

"Just allow your inhale to connect with the exhale in a circular manner like this," she said as she demonstrated. "Now close your eyes and allow yourself to relax into your breathing."

Abel closed his eyes. He picked up the rhythm of circular breathing and followed her voice and she guided him into a state of altered consciousness. Images came into his mind of swimming in an ocean all alone. He remembered his baptism, how he almost drowned. There was a tingling sensation that started in his hands and went up his arms. Soon he was tingling all over.

Abel could hear Darcy saying something. "Breathe," she said. "Keep breathing. As long as you're breathing, you're living. Don't worry; you're safe and immortal right now."

Then it happened. A shot of electricity like cocaine ran through his body and he broke into deep sobbing from his soul. There was a pain in his arm and he flashed back to being a junkie, kneeling in an alley shooting dope, blood dripping down his arm.

White cosmic light awakened him to a new level of consciousness and he let go of the sadness. Then the light in his head turned purple and he started to come back into the room. He had been reborn.

He thanked Darcy with a long, passionate hug and gave her the $50 that her service required. He spent the rest of the day re-reading Reawakening and

Rebirth and drinking ginseng tea. He was free. He was finally free.

Abel threw away the flowers and checked into a downtown hotel. He spent the night alone in his room contemplating his fate.

The next morning, he sat in a fast food joint waiting for them to come and pick him up. He knew they would be coming by. Downtown Goshen was always part of the morning blitz. He waited and drank coffee until they came and got him.

He had a long talk with Donald, his area captain. Abel told him about the guilt he suffered from some of his misadventures in the bush country, and Dennis put him on a plane bound for Moriah.

Abel arrived back at the Moriah MMT headquarters, located just outside the city limits on an as isolated ranch. They were all gearing up for a church holiday known as the Day of Truth in which they honored Father Truth by making a big meal and saying special prayers of offering and thanksgiving. Abel couldn't get into the spirit of celebration and he knew he didn't belong there anymore.

He left early in the morning before they woke up. He left a note on the kitchen table explaining that he had to move on to something else, he didn't know what. He threw his duffle bag full of clothes over his shoulder, jumped over the back fence, and took off into the wet winter night. It was raining, but he just kept running toward the highway. He knew that he had to get away soon before the others came looking for him. He stuck out his thumb as headlights approached. It was getting near dawn as a car finally pulled over and gave him a ride to downtown Moriah.

Abel rented a locker at the bus station and thought about where he wanted to go. He had about $300, which was enough to get him back to Eden Valley or back into Goshen where he thought that he could try it on his own. No, it was too cold for Wilderness this time of year.

He called home. He hadn't talked to his mom in over a year. She told him that she had been praying for him but that she knew he would be okay.

She suggested that it wasn't a good idea for him to come back to Eden Valley. She told him that he'd probably just get back with the same old friends again and start doing the same thing again, ending up back in trouble again.

"Have you considered just staying there in Moriah?" she asked.

"I've been thinking about a lot of things and maybe that's just what I'll do. I'll just stay here for a while and try to get a job. I know I'm a good salesman. I'm sure I can get a job somewhere. I have enough money to last me for at least a month. That ought to hold me."

"Well good luck," she said.

"Good-bye." He hung up the phone and looked out at the Moriah skyline, the skyscrapers pointing toward heaven.

CHAPTER 16

REAWAKENING

✳

In a rebirth
As children
Of the one Heart
Let our love
Embrace the earth.

Abel walked up the hill where he found a hotel that rented rooms for $65 a week. He gave the manager enough to cover his rent for the next two weeks, and hoped the rest would last until he got a paycheck from somewhere. At least he had a place to stay for now, he thought.

He ordered an all you can eat salad and a cup of water from Wendy's, and went back to the salad bar four times. That became his routine for a while since he had grown accustomed to vegetarian food when he was with the Truthies.

Abel headed to the library to do some reading. There he could feel safe. Somehow, he knew that just the right book would help him solve all of his problems. He grabbed a stack of books on cults and new religions and found a quiet corner with a soft chair and a big table. He thumbed through the books one by one and looked up all the references to the Truth Church. By the end of the day, he had convinced himself that leaving the church was the right thing to do. Still, there was that nagging doubt.

He called Darcy, the woman who had reawakened him in Moriah, and asked her to give him a referral to someone locally. She gave him the name of a woman named Stephanie. He gave Stephanie a call and arranged to see her the following day.

He took the bus out to Stephanie's large two-story house in a nice section of Moriah where she lived with her boyfriend, Houston. The process was much less traumatic this time and Stephanie suggested that he come back regularly for a series of ten sessions.

"This will help you get rid of all the lingering effects of your birth trauma and allow you to begin processing in new thought patterns."

"New thought patterns?" he asked.

She talked to him about practicing affirmations for a while and asked if he had read *Think and Grow Rich*. He told her that he had. She suggested that he also read *Birth Without Violence* by Dr. Frederick

Leboyer and a series called *The Life and Teachings of the Masters of the Far East.*

Birth Without Violence described the experiences of an unborn child as it traveled through the birth canal into a room of cold tables, bright lights and metal instruments. It also talked about the value of bonding with a newborn child and how new birthing techniques could result in healthier children.

Life and Teachings of the Masters of the Far East described a group of ascended masters called the "Great White Brotherhood" who dwelt among the Himalayas and controlled world events. Among them were Buddha, Mohammad, Confucius and Jesus. These ascended masters had all become enlightened through secret techniques and had developed superior mind power through affirmations and creative investigation. The books went on to describe how each of them were really gods with the same unlimited power and potential of the Almighty.

Abel got a job at Pat's Shoe Store, located on the corner of Second and Spike, a frequent haunt of street preachers, drug dealers and hookers.

The owner was a short, bearded man with jet-black hair, glasses and a bit of a potbelly. He introduced himself as Pat and told him that he was looking for a new salesman. Someone he could train.

Abel took Pat up on his offer. He didn't have any experience in retail sales, but he was desperate for a job, anything to keep him afloat. It seemed like an excellent opportunity at the time.

He started the next day bright and early. He didn't have a lot of clothes but he put on the best things that he had. "Don't you have any ties?" Pat asked. Abel told him that he didn't and Pat offered to bring him in a couple of ties the next day.

It felt good making an honest buck for a change. He thought about the thousands of dollars that had gone through his hands during the last year as he had lied, cheated and conned people. Whether to support his drug habit or his religious cause, it didn't matter. He knew he had done wrong.

He was still angry at the Truth Church. He felt used. He was glad that he had escaped. But something inside him was nagging at him as though he had done something wrong. Why was he still holding onto his leather-bound copy of the Divine Truth and his picture of Father Truth?

He decided to write a letter to Mr. Guerra, his former commander. He told him how he felt about all the work he had done for them and that he thought it wasn't fair that he didn't get paid for any of his work. He left them the number of an answering service and the address of a local mail drop.

The following week, he received a call from Francis, a member of Moriah MMT asking if she could meet him for lunch.

They met at a busy place on the Wharf and she treated him to a plate of nachos. She told him that the commander regretted his leaving the team, and would love him to come back.

Abel told her that he had made a firm decision regarding leaving the church. He just needed to resolve some feelings about all the uncompensated work he had done for True Products.

"How much do you feel they owe you?" she asked.

"About twenty-four hundred," he replied. He had based his figure on a minimum wage, forty-hour workweek over the four-month period that he had worked for the church's True Products Division. He knew that the church had maintained records on that particular income and he figured they didn't want to chance a lawsuit.

Francis delivered the money to him in cash at his job in three payments. The first time, she brought it to him right at the counter as Pat looked on with suspicion. He probably thought it was some kind of drug deal as he watched Francis counting out stacks of small bills totaling $635. He used the money to open up a checking and savings account at the People's Bank around the corner.

He went back to see Stephanie, his reawakener. The next session was powerful. The tingling sensation filled his body and he experienced distinct memories of his birth. Afterwards, they talked about various modes of therapy and she told him THAT was having a training sessions.

THAT stood for Thompson Holistic Attitude Training. In 1980, it seemed that everybody was getting THAT. THAT was a combination of Zen

Buddhism, Scientology, Primal Therapy and Hypnosis. It was marketed as a two-weekend course in enlightenment.

Stephanie told him the training was going to be held during the next two weekends, and that he needed to sign up right away if he wanted to attend. The fee was only $350 so he thought it was a good deal for the promise of enlightenment. He really needed as much help as he could get.

He also started looking through the paper for rooms to rent. Pat noticed that he had the classified section out one morning and asked if he was looking for another job already. He told him that he was just looking for a place that rented out cheap rooms. He mentioned that he and his wife were renting out a room in their house for $100 a month. The price was right so he decided to check it out. He showed him the room and told him that it would be no problem for him to give him a ride to work in the mornings. It was right on the bus line so he could take the bus anywhere he needed to go.

Abel moved into Pat's place the next day. Pat's wife was a genius and member of the Mensa Society. She worked at Jack in the Box.

She had a daughter from a previous marriage who said she had the power to move objects with her mind. Her parents had admonished her to quit doing it, however, because it was "of the devil."

***

The trainer would stand in the front of the rented hotel ballroom and call everybody "jackasses." He would badger, belittle and bully them into accepting the worldview of Morris Thompson, the former real estate salesman and founder of THAT. "Getting THAT" was the carrot and stick of enlightenment, which supposedly resulted from completing the two week training. At one point in the seminar, the trainer stood in the front of the room and yelled, "It ought to be perfectly clear to everyone that you are all jackasses and I'm God. Only a jackass would argue with God!"

The basic philosophy came down to this: "What is is; what is not is not." The sound of one hand clapping was simply the sound of one hand clapping. According to Thompson, "All of us are gods who came to Earth to play and forgot who we really were." Supposedly, we were all perfect beings with barriers to the full experience and expression of our perfection. "Wake up!" the trainer shouted.

Abel went to the THAT training that weekend which was being held in a large hotel ballroom. The trainer refused to allow participants to go to the bathroom once they were seated and the next break wasn't until noon when they broke for lunch. A woman in the back of the room wet her pants and started crying about halfway through the morning session. The trainer yelled at her to shut up and called her "a self-centered, attention-seeking little brat."

Finally, it was time to break for lunch and a buxom Creole girl invited him to have lunch with her. He couldn't refuse. She was stunning. They fell in lust at McDonald's over a fish sandwich and a quarter-pounder with cheese. Her name was Donna and her hair fell in silky dark russet waves around the face of an angel.

Abel sat alone in his room that night and thought about Donna. There was something deep and spiritual about her that attracted him more than even her generous cleavage, although the latter definitely had their place. He decided not to call her for a couple of days, even though he could tell she wanted to see him.

He finally broke down and called her and she invited him over. They spent the night together. Donna became his new drug of choice. She became a part of him and throughout the second weekend of the training, they were inseparable. He spent almost every evening at her house. She worked at Luigi's, a fancy seafood restaurant, as a waitress and would often bring him home a plate of the catch of the day.

Sometimes when he spent the night alone in his room, he would lay awake at night just thinking about her. He wondered what it was that made this relationship so intense. Perhaps it was the year and a half that he had just spent in a religious cult.

He still had unresolved feelings about the church. One night as he was eating dinner with Pat's family, there was a knock on the door. "It's for you," Pat said.

Abel went to the door and there stood Mr. Guerra. He asked if they could go somewhere and talk for a little while. Abel went with him to a little seafood place near the Pike and listened as he tried to convince him to come back to the church. Abel tried not to offend Mr. Guerra as he explained his reasons for leaving and his feelings about Father Truth.

He returned home, tore up the pictures of Father Truth, and burned his copy of the Divine Truth. It was over. He was free.

Abel and Donna went to see Hall and Oats in concert the following weekend. They spent the rest of the weekend in bed together. She told him how her last boyfriend had been a born-again Christian who was always quoting the Bible to her and trying to get her to give her life to Christ. She, like Abel, believed that Christ was already within each one of them and that they didn't need salvation from Jesus. Her last guru was Cashneesh, who owned a fleet of Bentleys and an entire rural town in Washington State. She told him that she never became a full member because she didn't like to wear orange. Cashneesh made all his disciples wear bright orange to symbolize the sunrise.

Morris Thompson was their new savior. They enrolled in a THAT follow-up seminar called "This is THAT," a 10-week series on processing anger and resentment. They were strongly encouraged to bring guests so they could sign up for the training.

A few days later, Abel was downstairs in his rented basement room at Pat's. He had just written another poem to Donna when Pat knocked on his door.

Pat stood there with a gallon bottle of wine in his hand. Abel invited him to come in and could tell he was drunk. Pat started complaining about how his wife had been bitching at him and how she wasn't treating him the way he wanted to be treated. Abel listened reluctantly for a while and interspersed the conversation with an occasional comment to let him know that he was paying attention to what Pat was saying.

Then the conversation began to take a weird twist. "I'd really like it if you would give me a back rub," Pat said.

Abel looked at him in disbelief. "Have your old lady do it," he said.

"That's my problem," Pat replied. "She won't do anything I ask her. She's being a bitch." He took a swig out of his wine bottle and sat down next to Abel on the bed. Abel could see that it was time to get rid of him.

"Pat," he began, "I can see that you've had too much to drink and you need to get some sleep. So, why don't you just go back upstairs to your wife?"

Then Pat started telling Abel how attractive he thought he was and how he hadn't had those kinds of feelings for a long time. Abel tried his best to convince him that he wasn't into men and that he already had a girlfriend.

"You think I'm a queer don't you?" Pat asked.

"Hey, whatever you're into that's your business."

"I could really make it good for you. Just let me show you." Pat started unbuttoning his shirt.

"Don't do this Pat," he said, "You're only going to piss me off and you don't want to do that. I told you already, I'm not into having sex with men." He stood up and gestured toward the door.

Pat stood up and began to walk away. Then he stopped for a minute and hung his head down. "Can I just tell you one thing?" he asked, "It would mean a lot to me if you'd just let me explain one thing."

Against his better judgment he said, "Go ahead. But make it quick, I'm getting tired."

Pat proceeded to tell him about an operation he had had about five years ago, an operation that transformed him from a woman into a man. He opened his shirt all the way and he could see the incision marks where her breasts had been removed. "Let me show you the rest," he said as he started to unzip his pants.

"No way!" Abel shouted angrily. He opened the door and told pointed the way out. Pat left.

Abel found an apartment in the University section of town and moved in the following weekend. Pat and Abel still worked together for another week and then Pat made up an excuse to fire him. Abel knew that it was time to move on anyway so he was relieved when Pat told him to turn in his shoehorn.

Donna expressed mixed emotions about his sudden change of circumstances. She was glad that he had his own apartment, but she felt a little insecure about him not working. Abel assured her that he had enough money in the bank to live on until he found another job. In the meantime, he told her that he was training to become a reawakener.

Abel sought counsel from a psychic astrologer who told him that he was born under an auspicious new moon. "Not only do you have a 'Grand Water Trine'," she said, "but I see you've also got a cross configuration that makes your destiny one of great prominence." She went on to tell him that he would be a great communicator in the areas of finance and religion, and that he would be doing a great deal of traveling and public speaking. "Be careful though," she warned, "With that double Pisces and Scorpio rising, you could be easily sidetracked by drugs and alcohol."

"I've already been through all that," he told her, "I'm on a natural high these days. I get high on breathing."

"Just be careful," she repeated.

The 10-week "This is THAT" seminar was ending and Donna and Abel were noticing a strain in their relationship. He told her that he didn't want to do any more seminars because he thought that THAT was just another cult. She got offended. "Morris

Thompson is the most important person on the planet," she said. "How you can sit there and degrade anything he created is simply beyond comprehension. He's the only one on the planet who's really making a difference."

Their relationship ended as suddenly as it had begun. One day, she just told him that things were no longer right between them. She told him that she needed space to work out a few things. Abel tried to convince her that they were meant to be together since the beginning of time. They had lived past lives together. Their horoscopes intertwined in perfect harmony. They had been through the training together.

He wrote her one last poem and lay in the bathtub filled with water and cried deep sobs of grief. Loneliness and abandonment embraced him as he cried himself through another reawakening.

CHAPTER 17

WEEKEND ENLIGHTENMENT

✳

When we first met
Winter was finally over
And much too cold
To keep around anymore
Spring began
This time a new beginning
An awakening from the long darkness
Our eyes met
And in stunning shyness
Glanced away.
Then turned again to gaze
With longing and remembering
Into the face of God

Abel's heart was still aching from the loss of Donna when he went to the next seminar. It was called the, "Weekend Enlightenment Training" or WET, and was being promoted as the feminine version of THAT. WET was centered on learning to love yourself before you could love another human being. It was created by Raylene Divine, one of the earliest pioneers of the reawakening movement, and incorporated the philosophy of physical immortality. Oscar Kilgore discovered reawakening after falling asleep in a sauna and waking up in an infantile state.

The original reawakeners used hot tubs and snorkels to induce memories of being in the womb. Later, Oscar discovered that it was the conscious breathing technique that actually caused the reawakening experience. Reawakening was promoted as the ultimate cure for the central problems of humanity known as the Five Biggies — Birth Trauma, Unconscious Death Urge, Parental Disapproval Syndrome, Specific Negatives, and Other Lifetimes.

The philosophy of physical immortality was at the heart of the reawakening movement. Raylene and Oscar were devotees of a guru named Poopooji who lived in the village of Udon Thani in Thailand. Poopooji was an immortal being, the incarnation of the King of Siam, and a Mahavator, or Greater Savior. According to legend, Poopooji had existed prior to the creation of the earth and had always returned in various forms during critical periods of cosmic evolution. According to Oscar, the Bible referred to Poopooji as Melchizedek, King of Salem, without father and mother. He was the one to whom Abraham paid tithes after returning from a great battle victory.

According to Poopooji, the supreme sound of the universe, or mahamantra, was, "OWATANA SIAM," which was supposed to vibrate with the essence of the five elements --earth, air, water, fire and ether.

Raylene and Oscar had visited Poopooji on several occasions, as had many other advanced seekers of spiritual enlightenment. They integrated the knowledge they brought back into the reawakening movement, the philosophy of physical immortality and the Weekend Enlightenment Training (WET).

Thought is creative and I am the thinker. That was the central theme of spiritual psychology. The universe was nothing more than thoughts made real. By changing their thoughts, they could change their reality. They were gods in their own universe, masters of their lives and destinies. Nobody could control them without their permission.

According to Oscar and Raylene, all problems began at the moment of birth when a person went from the safety, sufficiency and security of the womb to the danger, scarcity and uncertainty of the outside world. Out of this birth trauma came such proverbial thoughts as, "I can't get enough," "something's wrong with me," "I'm no good," "if this is life, then I don't want any part of it." Humans fell from their garden paradise ever blocked from returning by the flaming sword of truth.

The unconscious death urge was the direct result of a person's immediate reaction to life. Freud called it Thanatos. It was an urge to retreat to the womb, which manifested itself in all kinds of destructive and compulsive behavior. Since God placed them into a painful existence out of which the only escape was death, they were resentful toward God. Man rebelled. Satan was their standard-bearer.

Parental Disapproval Syndrome (PDS) was the name given to the guilt and inferiority complex most people received from their parents. "You were taught from an early age that your bodies were not to be touched, that they were bad, sex was dirty, and money was the root of all evil," said Raylene. "I'm going to show you how to free yourselves from PDS by using positive affirmations and creative visualization."

Affirmations were positive statements stated aloud in the first person present tense. Based on the principle that thought is creative; they were taught that they could create their own reality by affirming what they desired to be, do or have. Specific negative thoughts such as, "I can't get enough," were replaced with affirmations such as, "I now have abundance in my life" or "there is enough for everybody."

Raylene said, "The right affirmations will even conquer death, the last enemy." She told the seminar participants that, the thought that death was inevitable caused more deaths than all other causes combined. All death was suicide, a grave mistake, and always fatal. "If you can't take it with you, don't go," she shouted, cupping her hands to her mouth as if she was using a megaphone for emphasis.

During the last break, Abel met a woman from Canada who gave him her address and phone number and invited him to come up and visit her. Her name was Regina and she lived in Discover, Canada, just a few hours drive from Moriah. Regina was twenty years older than Abel, with short wavy blonde hair, a royal upturned nose, and the slender build of a ballet dancer. He promised to see her soon.

Abel was down to his last $100 and doing some desperate job hunting. He had applied for every kind of job he could think of from waiter to sales to drug counselor. The Employment Development Department denied his unemployment insurance claim from his last job and he was waiting for a decision regarding his appeal.

Regina lived in a large, Victorian house with another couple named John and Ariel. Everyone in the household made a practice of walking around the house totally nude. It took him a few minutes to get used to the idea, but he went along with the program without complaint. One morning, Ariel walked into the bathroom to brush her teeth just as he was emerging from the shower. As he toweled himself dry, he couldn't help but notice her supple, 20-year old body in the mirror in front of him. It was hard to hide his obvious attraction as she gazed at him, seductively. He resisted the temptation and smiled at her as she finished brushing her teeth. Their eyes met again for a moment of longing before she turned and exited the bathroom. He took a deep breath and looked at himself in the mirror as he repeated his affirmations:

"I now have abundance in my life."

"I am good enough to have anything my desire."

"The divine plan of my life is now manifesting."

"I am safe and immortal right now."

The four of them spent the week together eating vegetarian cuisine and staying up late discussing the finer points of the philosophy of physical immortality and spiritual psychology. He learned that Regina was formally the lead soprano for the Canadian Royal Opera as she showed him a room full of trophies, medals, commendations, and photographs of days gone by. She also told him that she had been a witch in a previous lifetime.

Abel had recently become lovers with a woman in Moriah named Diana who claimed to be a witch in this lifetime. She would sleep with a book of numerology under her pillow and she liked to make him meals mixed with strange herbs. He had met Diana at another seminar on physical immortality. She knew that he was in Discover to see another woman and she said it was okay with her. He often thought about her when he was with Regina.

> *My heart dances*
> *As the sound of the night*
> *Sings sweetly of romances, parting glances*

And of princes kissing hands
Of maidens
Gallantly, majestically,
My heart dances and dances and dances
To the rhythm of midnight.
My heart listens
To the song of the stars
As they glisten with their quiet light
They speak to me
So softly and so magically,
My heart listens, listens and listens
To the music of Heaven.
My heart dances
To the beat of the night
With wings of flame
As the angels take flight above the skies,
My heart dances and dances and dances
To the beat of "I love you."

Abel knew this thing with Regina wasn't going to last forever. She was 42, of royal blood and he was a 25-year old ex-junkie. She begged him to stay in Discover and offered to support him in every way for as long as he would stay with her. He contemplated her offer seriously for a moment, and then decided that his place for now was in Moriah. He needed to go back to his little apartment and wait for the divine plan of his life to manifest.

Abel slept with the witch Diana the night he returned to Moriah. She was asleep next to him when the phone rang the following morning. It was from a place called Jericho House, a residential drug abuse program where he had applied for work as a live-in drug counselor.

Ten minutes after he hung up the phone, it rang again. This time it was the unemployment office. They were sending him a check for two months back pay. He hung up the phone, turned to Diana and repeated his affirmation: "I now have abundance in my life." It was true.

The job at Jericho House required that he move in to a private room at the back of the house. Jericho House, or J-House as they called it, was located in downtown Moriah. It was a large, three-story Victorian house with offices, kitchen and living room on the first floor. The men lived on the second floor and the women on the third floor. The house maintained about twenty adult residents in a program lasting from six months to one year. Most of them were heroin addicts, some of whom were still on methadone maintenance or methadone detox. The staff kept the daily supply of methadone in the office safe.

The program relied mostly on group therapy, individual counseling, and behavior modification to provide treatment. J-House followed the traditions of Synanon and The Family and was heavily into confrontation and attack therapy. When Abel suggested the 12-step approach of Narcotics Anonymous, Dr. Alyse Devlin, the director, told him it was a bunch of religious nonsense that didn't work. "Besides," she said, "We don't want all those dope addicts from N.A. coming in here bringing drugs."

Dr. Devlin was a former English teacher from the Midwest who took the job at Jericho House because she needed the money. She had a doctoral degree in Education, but no experience at all regarding substance abuse. That was okay with him because he had plenty of experience with drugs, albeit little formal education. He had only completed a year and a half of college, although he put on his resume that he had a B.A. in Psychology.

The final interview went well and they asked how soon he would be ready to move in. He told them right away. He was already two weeks late on his rent, and he was down to his last $5. Diana helped him move in and they smoked a joint together in his new room to celebrate, careful to blow the smoke out the back door.

Dr. Devlin called the residents together in the group room and asked Abel to introduce himself.

He said, "I want you all to know that I believe in every one of you. Every one of you can make it. I've known people who've been to prison, been strung out on heroin and methadone for years, and are now clean and sober." He was really talking about himself.

Herb was the treatment director, a young Hispanic man, who was looking for a government job with the Department of Social Services. He was paying his dues by working in the trenches. Martha was the other counselor who had started working at J-House about two months before he did. She was a large, black Christian woman who sang in a church choir. She told him how she used to be hooked on pills when she worked for the probation department, until Jesus saved her. Abel tried to avoid her, knowing how much their theologies clashed.

Dr. Devlin assigned Abel to work with half of the clients in the house and he was responsible for leading three of the nightly confrontation groups. In his spare time, he continued going to seminars and lectures on various New Age topics.

He attended workshops in metaphysics, magic, meditation, mysticism, miracles, and mind over matter. Many of them were held at the Unity Church which he began attending, a blend of Christian Science, Science of Mind, and Eastern Metaphysics, which emphasized the principals of creative thought. "We create our own reality," was the church's motto and its seminars were always promoting New Age consciousness.

Meanwhile, he became deeply involved in reawakening, Tai Chi, yoga, meditation and many other spiritual disciplines. He was hooked on seminars. Books on the New Age, psychology and Eastern Mysticism lined his bookshelves. He studied Alice Baily, Aleister Crawley, Napolean Hill, Yogananda, Muktananda, Maharishi Mahesh Yogi, Cashneesh, L. Ron Hubbard, Marilyn Ferguson, Werner Erhard and countless others. He was addicted to learning more and more as he tried to fill the empty spiritual void that began to gnaw at his soul. He couldn't get enough. Everything seemed to be leading to nowhere, an endless abyss of cults and dark holes in space. He projected an image of having it all together, radiating perfect poise and calmness.

The Tai Chi helped him balance his male and female polarities, the yin and yang energy which flowed together in a cosmic dance throughout the universe. Tom Chow was his young Chinese instructor who was also a certified reawakener and creative writing teacher. He was also a devout follower of Poopooji.

Abel counseled his clients at Jericho House using many of the methods he had learned. The one thing that always seemed to help them was his ability to listen and acknowledge what they were saying and how they were feeling. He always suggested that they take a few deep breaths in order to relax and let go of stress. Then he would offer them a few appropriate affirmations and tell them to repeat them aloud twice a day in the mirror, "Every day in every way, I'm getting better and better," he said, "Now repeat it after me."

Peaches was a light-skinned half black, half Sebasto from Goshen who had been in and out of jail for prostitution and possession of narcotics. She looked at him and giggled as she tried to repeat the affirmation he had given her. There was a strong attraction between them, but he knew that he would have to resist if he wanted to keep his job, let alone his sanity and his sobriety. Besides, he still had Diana and Regina. He didn't need another girlfriend yet. He had an abundant life.

Diana soon became distant from him and he missed eyes looking back at his with longing. He had long since decided to become a professional reawakener and seminar leader, so he enrolled in the certification process. The requirements included being reawakened at least 10 times, giving seminars and completing numerous courses and training sessions.

He met Michelle at a seminar on Spiritual Psychology. She had long wavy brown hair and dark brown eyes that looked at him with déjà vu. They instantly realized they had gone through other lifetimes together. They became friends and lovers, and adventurers on the journey to physical immortality and enlightenment.

Michelle was a colonic irrigation specialist. He found the fact that she was a professional poop shoveler somewhat intriguing, exciting in a strange perverted way. When she told him this and described the process, he enrolled for 10 sessions with her. "It will purify your whole system," she beamed. Michelle was a strict vegetarian who believed that the cause of all the problems in the world was undigested red meat. It seemed to make sense at the time.

Once, as Michelle was performing a colonic on him, he mentioned a seminar on breathetarianism he had heard about. It was in Discover, Canada and they both decided it was something worth driving up there for.

They headed out in Michelle's Volkswagen, stopping along the way to do some magic mushrooms. "Why not, they're organic," he said. She agreed.

By the time they reached Discover, they were talking about the nature of thought and reality. "If I'm just a thought in the mind of God," she began, "what happens if God stops thinking about me?"

"We're all a part of God," he answered. "The only separation is illusion. In fact, the real original sin was the thought that we were separate from God."

They checked into the hotel and headed down to the conference center, where the breathetarianism seminar was getting started. There was electric excitement in the air as they anticipated the arrival of Fred Sawyer, noted breathetarian.

Abel waved to several acquaintances he had met from other seminars as Abel and Michelle found the only available seats. The person sitting next to them was Regina, the Canadian soprano. She was there with her new boyfriend. He tried to play it casual as he introduced her to Michelle but he found it strangely exciting to sit between two lovers during the lecture.

Fred Sawyer claimed he had not eaten solid food for the last 15 years. He also claimed to be able to lift over 1,000 pounds, which was no small feat for a 36-

year old man who only weighed 120 pounds. Fred was clean-shaven and about six feet tall with long blonde hair. His theory was based on the premise that man is a spiritual being sustained by the breath of life.

"Eating is an acquired habit like smoking cigarettes, taking drugs or drinking alcohol," he began. He went on to describe a worldview where man originally was made in God's image as a spiritual being. As man descended to earth, he lived on dew and sunlight. The original sin was the literal eating of the fruit of the tree that led to an experience of duality. Humans began to descend from breathetarians to fruitarians to vegetarians, and finally to the violent carnivores of today. The cause of all modern ills was tainted blood resulting from what we ate.

Man's purpose, according to Fred Sawyer, was to return to their original state of Edenic perfection by slowly returning to a breathetarian diet. Fred gave them an invitation to his weeklong seminar at Bailey Hot Springs in California. The cost of the seminar was $500. Michelle and he decided they had to go. This was what they knew they needed for the next level of their evolution.

Abel went back to work with his newfound knowledge and began arranging to attend Fred's weeklong seminar. He and Michelle had started talking about getting married and running off to Hawaii to live on dew and sunlight. She would start a business as a holistic health consultant and he would write poetry and philosophy.

Dr. Devlin didn't take well to the idea of Abel's sudden desire to leave Jericho House. When he talked with her further, they decided that what he really needed was just a weeklong vacation.

This would allow him an opportunity to attend the seminar and spend some time alone with Michelle before making any major decisions.

Michelle and Abel arranged to ride down to California with Lindsey and Tamara, a lesbian couple whom they both knew from previous seminars. They packed up a borrowed Volkswagen Bus and headed down the highway talking philosophy and drinking distilled water and lemon juice. They were on their way to becoming full-fledged breathetarians.

Bailey Hot Springs was located just sixty miles east of Babylonia. It was a newly furnished resort with a large cabin area. Abel and Michelle picked a couple of bunks in the corner and unpacked their belongings.

Outside were large pools of hot mineral water. Everyone took their clothes off and spent the breaks relaxing and frolicking in the sun. The meals were based on Fred's Golden Diet, a carefully selected list of foods that were supposed to give the body a golden aura. Sawyer created the yellow diet as a detoxification process and transition toward full breathetarianism.

Fred lectured them for hours on end about the values of the breathetarian lifestyle. He told them that it would reverse the aging process and they would end up with so much energy they would only need a couple of hours sleep each night. He told them to repeat the following affirmation: I am a spiritual being sustained by the breath of life. "Let it be your mantra," he said.

Before they left, Michelle picked up an ounce of marijuana from a stockbroker who attended the seminar. They had a major argument about it, but he finally agreed to let her take it back with them. The four of them headed back up the highway totally convinced that they were on the cutting edge of an evolution of consciousness about to take a quantum leap to a new plane of existence. They stopped along the way at a motel in Eugene, Oregon where Abel and Michelle relaxed in the hot tub. Michelle closed her eyes and smiled as the warm jets pulsated against her breathetarian body.

Michelle ended up moving in with Abel at Jericho House when she was kicked out of her house for smoking pot. Dr. Devlin agreed to let Michelle stay with him on a temporary basis. Within one month, they were on each other's nerves and then she started seeing somebody else, another one of her colonic clients.

When Michelle moved out of Jericho House, Abel's heart was broken. He covered up his pain with marijuana, which wasn't really a drug, he convinced himself. It was organic. He was still a drug counselor and he needed to keep himself cool. Abel and Michelle continued to see each other for a while but it wasn't the same after she moved away. He tried to pretend that it was okay for her to see other guys but he knew it wasn't.

Abel started getting closer to Peaches, but still resisted the temptation to go beyond the ethics of his profession. Several clients were using drugs and she was one of them. The staff ordered urinalysis for all the residents. Nearly half of them came back positive opiate, cocaine and marijuana. Peaches' test came back positive for all three. She and several other residents were kicked out of the program. Abel told her to call him if she needed anything.

He awoke one morning with a raging toothache, an impacted wisdom tooth. He went to the dentist who put him under with sodium pentothal. When Abel awoke, he felt groggy and his mouth was swollen and numb from the Novocain. The dentist gave him a prescription for 20 Percodans, a narcotic painkiller, which was stronger than codeine. The prescription was supposed to last almost a week. Two days later, Abel was back at his office begging for more. Reluctantly, the dentist gave him a prescription for eight more. "Be careful," he said, "These things are highly addictive."

"I know," he replied, "I'm a drug counselor." he took all eight of them the same day.

Percodan had a similar effect on him as a mild dose of heroin. A warm, euphoric sense of peace sprang from the inside out. He was back in the womb again. He smiled broadly, as he went back to Jericho House and greeted several clients on his way back to his room. He was already hooked again.

The next morning, he took a bottle of methadone from the safe. He drank half of it and filled it back up with Kool-aid. Afterwards, when the client drank it, she commented that it seemed weaker than usual.

He knew that it was time to move on to a new profession. He checked through the want ads and found a job as a commodities broker. He worked part-time and he arranged with Dr. Devlin to work at Jericho House on a part-time basis for a couple of months before he resigned from Jericho House completely.

An investigative reporter discovered Fred Sawyer sneaking into a 7-11 buying a burrito, a couple of candy bars and a pack of cigarettes. Lindsey and Tamara were heartbroken. Abel was disappointed and felt cheated again by another false guru. There were ripples of doubt and dissent throughout the reawakening community as the new clothes of emperors revealed their nakedness. Abel wanted out. He needed to focus on the things of this earth for a while.

CHAPTER 18

THE RAZOR'S EDGE

✶

This one was so special
Really precious
Something different
More than just her name
No there was much more
That set apart this one
From all the rest
Not just the way we met
Not just the way we came
Together on a January night.
No there was much more
So much more
About this one
This precious one
This oh so special one
This only one.
This one and only one.
Who was the way she was
Only she

Did what she did to me
She was the only one
Who touched me there
The only one I would let so close
So close
She came
And then I came
And then we came.
We both knew this was more
Much more
Much more than just a game
And that the difference was much more
Than just her name.
Much more.
Much more.

Abel worked part time job at King Sun Commodities, located in the heart of Moriah's Chinatown and owned by an international corporation based in Hong Kong. They bought and sold gold contracts on the London and Hong Kong markets using a variety of strategies. Everybody had a different system of determining when to buy or sell. The technicians or chartists relied on charting the past performance of the market and looking for patterns in the rising and falling prices. If, for example, the chart showed that gold had dipped twice, then it would be due for a sudden upturn. That would be an indicator to "go long" or buy at the present low price with the expectation that it would go up. Slight movements in price could yield a client thousands of dollars of which the broker would receive a generous commission.

Fundamentalists relied on world events, business news and other fundamental factors to affect the price of gold. For example, if a war was starting to break out, people would begin hoarding gold and the price would go up. Other fundamentalists relied on more esoteric factors such as the fall of the I Ching, astrology, or the way the goldfish were swimming in the fish tank. If the fish were swimming at the bottom of the tank, the price of gold was down, so it was an opportunity to buy very low. If the goldfish were swimming near the top of the tank, it would indicate that they should sell short, or bet that the market was heading for a downturn.

Another system was based on the phases of the moon. The assumption was that human emotions were influenced by the moon's gravitational pull just like the tides. During a full moon, people were likely to spend money more freely, leading to rising prices. The new moon would influence people to act out of a sense of scarcity, thus causing prices to fall.

Sound of Immortality
Long silent whispers
Of the western wind
With your sweet embrace,
Carry me, gently
Home again.

Song of life's renewal
Eternal mantra
Of the highest Heaven
Where the master dwells,
The still small voice within
Holy of Holies.
Mother of the seven seas
Embrace me
In your Great white cosmic noise
Like waterfalls,
Return me
To the source.
Sound of immortality
Rebirth me
In the breath of life divine,
Awakening the seed that is my soul
To everlasting life.

Abel was now living in an apartment in the University District. His friend Kali, whom he had met at a reawakening workshop, was going to Thailand to meet with the guru Poopooji, and she let him have all of her furniture. He told her he would pay for it when he got settled. Kali told him she would be gone for at least a month and not to worry about paying for the furniture until she got back. She invited him to come to Thailand with her but he declined.

Abel still believed in Poopooji as the incarnation of the King of Siam and as the greatest immortal being on the face of the earth. He had been the one who had convinced Kali of who Poopooji really was. "What is Poopooji's relationship to Jesus?" she had asked.

"During the last years of Jesus' life," Abel began, "between the ages of 13 and 30, Jesus traveled to Egypt, India and Tibet to study under the great masters including Poopooji. There he learned the secrets of immortality and healing. Poopooji, in fact, is Jesus' father."

"That blows me away," said Kali. "I still don't know why I should ever want to go to Thailand. Why do you want to go there?" she asked.

"For the same reason the Kundalini wants to reach the crown chakra," he replied.

"I see," said Kali.

Abel and Kali became lovers and friends from the night they first met. She understood that he was involved in multiple primary relationships and she said it was okay with her.

Now she was leaving him all of her furniture and flying off to Thailand to visit God. Abel wanted badly to just forget about everything else and go with her, but he knew that he had to stay. Besides, he felt that Poopooji had already given him the secret of immortality in the form of the Mahamantra, "OWATANA SIAM," which reverberated constantly in his head. Immortality was his birthright as Poopooji and he were one in spirit and in truth.

Abel got a postcard from Kali about a week later telling him that just before she arrived in Udan Thani,

Poopooji, the immortal being, had a heart attack. He died on Valentine's Day, 1983. "What a sense of humor he has," she wrote. Abel filled his bathtub with water, laid back until the water came just below his chin and chanted the mantra, OWATANA SIAM repeatedly, emphasizing different syllables, repeating it slowly and loudly until he finally realized its true meaning: OH WHAT AN ASS I AM!

Before he left Jericho House, Abel got a call from Peaches, the client he had kicked out of the program about a month previously. She was trying to get into another program and wanted to know if he could help her. He agreed to make some calls for her.

Abel and Peaches talked on the phone several times during his last days at Jericho House. Finally, she invited him to her house where she lived with her stepfather and 5-year old son, Dell. He took her out to a trendy nightclub on University Avenue. They ordered pasta with clam sauce and drank white wine until closing time.

She confided that her stepfather had tried to molest her several times and that she needed to get out of there. Abel let her spend the night at his house as they decided on a plan of action. It turned into a night of unabashed passion. As a former prostitute, Peaches knew how to do things in bed that he had never even imagined. He was hooked from the first night they were together. He had to have her always. They drank wine, danced to the music of DeBarge, and partied throughout the night.

Within a week, he had let Peaches and her son Dell move in with him. After little Dell peed off the balcony, Abel had her make arrangements to let him live with his father. Then Ginger moved in. Ginger was a friend of Peaches, who still worked as a hooker. "This is the only job I've ever had where I could get paid for doing what I love," she said. They all got along fine. Everything Peaches asked for Abel gave her. She suggested that he invest a few hundred dollars into a couple pounds of high-grade marijuana so they could supplement their incomes. He agreed and before long he was smoking and dealing weed while Peaches worked as a stripper, and Ginger turned tricks in a whorehouse. He quit his commodities broker job and starting pimping and dealing full-time. Everything was going great and they were partying every night, dancing, drinking, smoking weed until dawn.

Then came the pills. Just a couple of Valiums at first, then Ritalin and Codeine. "They're a lot better if you shoot them up," Peaches suggested. Zap! Electric Avenue. He was stoned again and wanting more. Then came Dilaudid, a potent synthetic narcotic that was as powerful as heroin, if not more so.

"Forty dollars apiece for number fours," she told him. He bought two of the little pills, crushed them into a spoon, added water, and split it three ways with the girls. Smacked back to the max, his chin was in his chest. "This was the Heaven I had lost," he said, "I'm home again."

Within a month, Abel was strung out again on heroin and cocaine. He started demanding more money from the girls and they were starting to hold out on him because of their own growing habits. They missed the rent payment. The girls split and he was on his own. Strung out bad, he was waking up sick every morning. He drained his bank accounts and maxed out his credit cards. He was down to living on unemployment insurance and he knew that life was falling apart quickly.

Abel started hanging out in shooting galleries down around an area of town called the Razor. The Razor was a predominantly black area of town where drugs and sex were sold openly. He gave a guy a ride to pick up some dope and the guy turned Abel on to enough stuff to start dealing. He started selling heroin in the shooting galleries and he would sometimes run into his former clients from Jericho House. They were always glad to see him because they knew that he would give them a good deal. He was ashamed of what he was doing, and what he had become, but he couldn't help himself. He was a junkie.

One day, Abel ran into the shooting gallery to see if he could sell a few balloons of dope. One guy said he wanted to buy two bags for $30. "No problem," Abel said as he spit the bags out of his mouth and set them on the table in front of him.

"Well, how about just giving me five bags for $50, can you do that," he asked.

"Okay man, here," he said. Abel spit out his last three bags. Fifty dollars would give him just enough to go pick up again. He already had about $200 on him.

He flashed the money in front of Abel and scooped up the bags. Then he put the money back in his pocket and tried to walk away.

"Wait a minute," Abel began.

Before he could finish the sentence, about five guys were on top of him. They punched and kicked him from every direction. He swung back wildly as he made his way out of the front door and tumbled down the steps onto the front lawn. Abel could feel somebody grabbing his wallet and his money clip as he tried to crawl out to the street where his car was parked.

He finally made it to his car. He was barefoot, broke and bleeding. He drove around the corner with squealing tires as he made his escape. There was an eviction notice on his door when he arrived. He cleaned himself up and laid there watching television with an ice pack over his swollen cheek. A commercial came on. The voice over sang, "Be All That You Can Be, In the Army!"

CHAPTER 19

BE ALL THAT YOU CAN BE

✻

March on
As a god of war
Head held high
Toward the stars.
March on
Young soldier with a mission,
March on!

Move out
Beyond the emptiness,
Let rain conceal your loneliness,
March on
With single vision,
Complete the mission!

Charge forth
Beyond your body's pain.
Forget about the wind and rain
March on

With calloused feet
Until the mission is complete.

Forward march
Through silent screams
Through broken bones
And shattered dreams.
March on
Beyond the agony
Of war's insanity.

March on
Past your final breath
And leap beyond the veil of death
When freedom reigns beneath the sun
Your mission on this earth is done.
March on!

Abel joined the Army as an alternative to suicide. He just wanted to be anything but the lowlife, strung-out junkie he had become. He packed up his car with all his belongings and headed south to California.

The recruiter gave him a rundown on the basic options available to him and mentioned that the Army had a two-year enlistment plan available. Abel told the recruiter that he was on his way to California to visit his family but that he was definitely interested in joining. The recruiter suggested that he wait until he got to California to sign up because of all the testing and paperwork.

About halfway through Oregon, his car started leaking oil and smoking badly. He had to stop about every hundred miles to add a couple of quarts of oil. By the time he reached Babylonia, his car was falling apart. The transmission went out.

Abel took the bus to the Army recruiter's office. He took the tests and the physical and passed everything with top scores. He signed up under the Army's Delayed Entry Plan, which meant he didn't have to leave until the end of February, 1984. That would give him Thanksgiving, Christmas, New Years and his birthday to enjoy with his family whom he hadn't seen in five years.

He completed all the processing for his military enlistment. He was praying that they wouldn't come across his criminal record or drug history. He signed up for a statewide assignment as a unit supply specialist so he wouldn't need a security clearance of any kind.

Abel got a job at Central City Jewelers. They needed some extra help in their sales department during the Christmas season and he convinced them he was an excellent salesman. They had him take a lie detector test that he was able to pass by shooting a quarter gram of heroin and lying on every question. His responses were consistent.

In the meantime, he started hanging out with some of his old friends again. Jay Hanuman gave him the rundown on what had happened to most of the old gang. Jay's sister Grace was going to nursing school. Yogi had been gang raped in prison but had found protection by joining the Los Vatos Locos. Jay was dealing for the Crypto Surf Nazis who distributed heroin out of Babylonia. Jay started trading Abel mass quantities of heroin for all the gold and diamonds he could get his hands on. Within one month, Abel had a two hundred dollar a day habit.

He knew he was going to have to quit before it was time to go into the Army. He got back on methadone for a 21-day detox. He also started taking massive doses of Vitamin C and B-complex to detoxify his system. He went through a week of misery before he finally kicked the habit. A local acupuncturist helped him with a series of strategically placed needles to relieve stress and boost his levels of beta-endorphins and serotonin.

One day Yogi showed up at Central City Jewelers. Abel didn't recognize him at first because of he had lost so much weight.

They met after work and Yogi told him he had been selling speed for Los Vatos Locos. He showed Abel a fistful of hundred dollar bills to prove it to him. They shot up some speed together and he got so wired up that Abel needed some heroin to bring him back down to reality. Within one week, his dope habit was raging out of control.

The Christmas rush was now over and the manager fired Abel from his job. "You just don't belong here," she told him, "You're like a square peg in a round hole," she said.

Abel took his last paycheck and spent it all on heroin. The day of his military departure was closely approaching and he knew that he would have to do something to get off this dope again. He decided to just lock himself up in his room for a few days and go cold turkey. He told his family that he had the flu.

When the day of his departure finally arrived, Abel he took a bag of clothes and a few books and got on the Greyhound bus back to Angel City. He had about $50 to his name. He was hoping it would last him until he got his first Army paycheck. He was still feeling week from withdrawal systems when he got on the bus. The young hippie girl in the seat next to him smiled as Abel drifted off to sleep.

When he got off the bus in Angel City, he discovered that the cash in his pockets was gone and he was penniless. Fortunately, he still had his wallet. He would need his ID to complete his final processing at the Military Entrance Processing Station.

Abel signed the final papers, raised his hand for the oath of allegiance, and boarded a bus heading toward the airport. He left California wearing a Members Only jacket. The weather was a clear 70 degrees and he was having cold sweats from heroin withdrawals. His nose ran and he choked on the bile that crept up his esophagus like an acidic drain opener. When he arrived in Ft. Ice, New York, he was backhanded across the face by a minus 20-degree winter. It was like taking a hot glass straight out of the dishwasher and placing it under cold running water. He thought his bones were going to shatter into a million little pieces.

Basic Training was one of the hardest things he had ever done. He was 28 years old, one of the oldest members in the unit and he was kicking a ten-year heroin habit. When he started Basic, he could barely do five pushups or run a block without puking his guts out. After eight weeks of grunting and sweating, he was finally able to do over seventy-five pushups at a time, and run two miles carrying an M-16 and full backpack. He learned how to take apart and put together an assortment of automatic weapons, crawl under barbed wire while machine guns fired overhead, set up minefields, and fire a light anti-tank weapon. He had become a warrior. At their graduation, Abel wore his dress green uniform proudly with the rank of Private First Class emblazoned on his shoulders as their company performed drill and ceremony in front of the commanding general. After the ceremony, they all got a pass to go up to the Post Exchange for beer and pizza.

A short, dark-haired woman caught his eye as he went up to the counter to order his second pitcher of beer. She was a PFC named Rachel and was transferring to Ft. Rex for Quartermaster School. Abel was heading to the same place and he was leaving the next day. They talked for hours as they drank beer and gazed into each other's eyes. She told him that she would meet him in Ft. Rex in two weeks.

Abel arrived in Ft. Rex and waited for Rachel to join him there. In the meantime, he called her often and sat up long lonely nights writing love poetry. She had become like a drug to him. This time it seemed like he had found something very special.

She arrived three weeks later. His training was nearly over and hers was just beginning. They were intimate at every opportunity, often sneaking away into the bushes for a quick romp. On the night of July 4th they were together behind Brigade Headquarters lying beneath the stars. The loudspeakers blasted Jimi Hendrix playing the Star Spangled Banner in the background. Then the fireworks exploded overhead in a spectacular display as their frenzied pitch exploded into oneness, leaving them breathless.

Then it came time for them to receive their assignments. He was hoping to God that Rachel and he would go to the same post. He ended up in Ft. Comfort, Washington. She went to Ft. Carson, Colorado. They stayed in touch for a while and even visited each other on a few occasions, but after awhile the magic finally wore off and he was alone again.

When he arrived at Ft. Comfort, the first thing they told them was to, "Stay off of Clinton Avenue. There's nothing but trouble there. Dope. Prostitutes. Nothing but trouble," the sergeant declared. Abel couldn't wait to find out for himself.

He was assigned to Headquarters Company, United States Army Garrison, or HHC USAG of the Last Infantry Division. This was the largest company at Ft. Comfort, responsible for administration, personnel and military justice. All of the JAG officers were assigned to Headquarters Company and they were responsible for certain military prisoners who could not be confined to the Stockade or Prisoner Control Facility for security reasons.

Abel's first assignment was the Central Issue Facility (CIF), where he gave out special equipment such as sleeping bags, cold-weather gear, helmets and survival equipment for soldiers who had to go to the field. Because of his administrative assignment, Abel only received an exercise uniform and a laundry bag. They called them a sham unit because they all had kickback jobs and never had to do field duty. That was okay with him.

CIF was located at the end of the post and their shifts were often irregular. As a result, everyone who worked there received an extra allowance for food and drinking, called separate rations and Basic Allowance Quarter (BAQ). Separate rations and BAQ came to about $400 a month, which was about half of his take home pay. It came in handy when he wanted to buy a car and keep the party going.

When they reassigned him to work in the supply room, he never told anyone he no longer needed the separate rations or BAQ, even though his new job was less than 100 feet from the barracks and the mess hall was right around the corner.

Rodney Jones was the specialist in charge of the supply room. He was a cool pothead from southern California who had gotten out of the service just a year ago, and had a hard time holding onto a regular job. "I got tired of pounding nails," he said, "So I decided to sign back up for another term."

Zelda came to their unit from the Personnel Control Facility. She was brought back as a deserter and was being held for court martial. While she was in custody, she reported that a guard had sexually assaulted her. The military police assigned her to Abel's unit while they were investigating the case. Rodney pointed her out to him and told him about her background.

Zelda was a tall blonde-haired woman with sparkling green eyes and an infectious smile. Abel knew the moment their eyes met that he had to have her.

Keep this to yourself," Rodney whispered, "I slept with her last night."

Abel laughed nervously, "How was she?" he asked.

"Amazing. I think I'm in love."

"Don't worry," Abel said, "your secret is safe with me, bro. Hope everything works out for you guys." He was determined to take her away from him.

That night, Abel took Zelda to a party off post. She told Abel that Rodney was a lame and denied ever having sex with him. Abel and Zelda began to spend more and more time together drinking, partying, and getting high. Two weeks later, she dropped the bomb on him. "I'm pregnant," she said. "But don't worry, it's not yours."

"Oh that's great," Abel said. Stinging from the shock of her announcement, he looked at her stomach and he could see the bulge. It was true.

"So, do you want to talk about it?" he asked. He hung his head down in disappointment not knowing if he really wanted to hear any more. He stayed and listened anyway.

Zelda told him that the stockade sergeant who raped her while she was in custody was the father. She told Abel that the pregnancy was too far along for him to have gotten her pregnant. Abel had only started being intimate with her a couple of weeks ago and she was already six weeks pregnant.

The sergeant in question was later court martialed, busted down to private and sentenced to six months in Leavenworth before receiving a dishonorable discharge. The sergeant's wife of six years filed for divorce. Zelda received leniency for her testimony and left the service without disciplinary action. After she had the baby, she called Abel and told him that the baby was really Rodney's and that she blamed it on the sergeant to get leniency in her own court martial. She never told Rodney he was the father.

BAM! BAM! BAM! It was four o'clock in the morning and somebody was banging on the barracks door. "Get up! Get dressed and stay out of the latrine!" the voice behind the door yelled. Abel panicked. It was a drug test and he, like many of his friends, had been smoking pot the night before. He grabbed a wine cooler from the portable refrigerator in their room and downed it in about five gulps. He figured that his first pee of the day would be the most toxic so he got rid of it in the only place he could. He filled the wine cooler bottle and set it in the trashcan.

He put on his uniform and headed downstairs to the dayroom after making sure he didn't leave any stash in the room. The MPs were already searching every room with German Shepherds while they sat and waited nervously eyeing each other with looks of impending doom.

If only there had been a little advanced notice, he could have prepared for this. A couple of day's abstinence and gallons of liquids combined with a little Golden Seal herb would have cleaned out his system nicely. He could have dropped a few crystals of powdered Drano into the urine bottle before he filled it. That would have neutralized any traces of illegal drugs.

The test came back positive for marijuana. The First Sergeant ordered him to go outside and shovel snow as they decided what to do next. After all, he had the keys to a weapons room filled with M-16 rifles and .45 caliber semiautomatic pistols, as well as access to hundreds of thousands of dollars worth of military equipment and supplies. He prayed for God to get him out of this one.

An hour later, the First Sergeant called him back into the office. Somehow, there had been a break in the chain of custody. Somewhere between the barracks and the testing lab, someone left the specimen bottles unguarded for a few minutes. Abel wondered if they were referring to when somebody asked him to keep an eye on the bottles for a minute and then he left them alone in the supply room to check out some weapons. Bottom line was the tests were invalid.

Everyone whose tests had come up positive would be retested within a couple of weeks. Abel told the First Sergeant that he didn't know how his came up positive in the first place. Someone either must have switched bottles on him or perhaps it was the time he was in the same room with some guys who lit up a joint. "Some of the smoke must have got into my system", he said with a straight face.

He knew then that he had to get out of the barracks. He stopped smoking pot long enough to pass the next urine test, but he was back at it the next night. Then some of them got together and bought a little coke. Before long, he was getting high every night.

He was hitting the local nightclub scene heavily. There was this placed called Broham's where a bunch of the guys would go for happy hour. Broham's had a big food bar loaded with fruit, salad, sliced, turkey, roast beef and about five different kinds of cheese. Best of all, they had two for one drinks so for about two bucks each they could eat like pigs and have a couple of beers to get them started for the night.

A few days later, he went down to Clinton Avenue and picked up a hooker. Her name was Roxie, a beautiful Eurasian with long brown hair and eyes that looked back at his with mystery. She, like most of the women on the street, was a heroin addict. Within a week, he was sharing an apartment with Roxie and shooting heroin five times a day, strung out again, with six months left before his Expiration Term of Service (ETS).

Abel finally decided to turn himself into the Army's drug and alcohol program. They put him in the hospital for a week and gave him a prescription for methadone. His counselor told him to get involved with a 12-step recovery group and find some other kind of creative outlet. "You've got a lot of potential, Abel," he said, "If you could just put as much energy into something positive as you do into your self-destructiveness, the stars would be yours."

Abel told his counselor that he had thought about being a writer but was afraid of failing.

"It's not failure you're afraid of. You're afraid of success. Deep down inside there's a part of you that knows how brilliant and creative you really are. But there's another part that's afraid to let your genius shine through. Forget about the future or the past," he said. "Just live in the now. If you want to be a writer, write. Just do the thing. Write."

Abel came back the following week and told the counselor that he had been thinking more about writing and had even checked out a couple of books on the subject from the post library.

"Don't just think about writing, talk about writing, or read about writing. If you want to write, then write, damn it, write!"

Ok, Ok. Abel started writing. He filled a journal with poetry and a myriad of ideas that now began to flow like water.

He survived the last few months of military service and moved to Angel City. He picked up a gram of heroin before leaving Ft. Comfort and shot it up at stops along the way. He had a blue Honda Accord with a U-Haul hooked to the back. Before he left, he tied his combat boots together, painted FTA – "FORGET THE ARMY" (or something to that effect) – on the bottoms of the soles and threw them over a telephone line where they hung behind the barracks as a symbol of his leaving.

CHAPTER 20

ANGEL CITY

✽

Bridges burn
As I leap
Quantumly forward
In faith
No turning back

Light shines
Out of darkness
Destiny homeward
In hope
Claiming the promise
Promised land

Out of the wilderness
Heavenly onward
In love
Safely home again.

Abel was all alone in Angel City with no money and no immediate prospects. His Aunt Delilah offered to rent him a furnished house for $500 a month. Abel gave her the last of his savings and moved in. He called up Max, who was trying to make a living as a musician, playing back up guitar for some of the local rock bands. Max got him a part as an extra in Tommy Tinsel's new movie, Tinsel Town Tussle. They also enrolled in a screenwriting course at the Angel City Scriptwriting Institute.

Cosmo was working as a film editor at Glorify Studios located at the Tinsel Studio lot in Cornerstone. He told Abel to check with personnel about getting an entry-level position. He applied and landed a job in the purchasing department as an administrative assistant. Glorify was producing some of the biggest prime time shows of the season and he would see the stars from those shows every day.

Max was living with a married woman from France named Bridgette. He told Abel that he needed to get some space in that relationship and asked if he would rent him his other bedroom. "Cool," he said. Max paid Abel enough to cover the rent for the whole place. He could cover the utilities with the money from his new job. Max had just received a large insurance settlement and paid for two months in advance.

"We oughta celebrate," he said. It had been years since they had partied together. Abel had been hard at work on a screenplay and needed a break.

Max was out front in his white '77 Cadillac. He jumped in the caddy and they rounded the corner of Las Brisas and Manford until they came to Saturnalia Drive. Three blocks away from where he lived was one of the biggest crack neighborhoods in Angel City. As soon as they turned onto the street a flock of young gang bangers descended on them like flies on dung, each of them displaying handfuls of the yellowish-white rock.

"Double ups!"

"Rock!"

"Got it good, homey."

"Primo, my brothers. Check it out."

"I got the biggest rock on the block."

The music from ghetto blasters was bumping and Max as Abel fell into the groove, mesmerized by the electric mood of the night.

"Just this one time," Max said.

"Yeah. Just this one time."

They picked up a twenty and stopped by a corner liquor store for the essential paraphernalia: rubbing alcohol, cotton balls, a glass pipe, a couple of screens, and a pack of razor blades.

They ran into the house with the speed of thieves and headed for the dining room table. Max set the rock on a mirror and cut it in half with a razor blade. He deftly placed a cotton ball on the end of a stretched-out coat hanger, dipped it in rubbing alcohol, and set it aflame with a butane lighter. He placed the pipe between his lips and slowly brought the torch above the bowl. The rock sizzled and popped as it melted into the pipe. Max took a long, slow drag, pulling the thick white curls of smoke through the glass. As his lungs expanded, Abel watched as Max's eyes bulged and beads of sweat appeared on his forehead. He exhaled the smoke in a slow steady sigh and he saw a look of wild intensity ignite Max's features, eyes gazing wildly into space.

"Lock the doors," Max said, his crack deluded psyche reeling in paranoid delusions. Abel knew this had to be some good stuff.

Abel put the other half in the pipe and took a hit. Boom! Electric Avenue ran up and down his spine transporting him instantly to Zap City. The sound of rushing water ran through his head, echoing like cellophane.

They continued taking turns hitting the pipe in a vain effort to recapture the exhilaration of that first blast, like chasing a rainbow. Abel scraped the pipe for resin as Max crawled around on the floor looking for a crumb that he was certain had fallen. They decided to get just one more rock so they could really feel it this time. This time they copped a fifty and swore again that this would be the very last time.

From that moment on, it was like a runaway freight train and they were both tied to the tracks. Abel tried desperately to regain that original high but it was like chasing a butterfly to the sun.

Before long, he was getting high at work, before work and after work. He carried the crack pipe around in his pocket and every time he had money, he spent it on rock. It started making him crazy.

When Abel got to work, his boss directed him to the personnel office to pick up his final paycheck. "Guess it just wasn't a match," the director said, shaking his head at his disheveled appearance.

He spent his final paycheck on crack. Weeks later he was wearing the same clothes, unshaven, wandering the streets before dawn looking for one more hit. Max and Abel continued on their self-destructive rampage until he woke up one evening to a nearly bare house, the rent was two months overdue and he owed over $5000 to Damon, the not so friendly neighborhood crack dealer. Max had disappeared and he was alone with the raging beast that was his tortured soul.

Abel knew that he shouldn't have opened the door that night. It was Damon, standing against the night sky, blacker than tar heroin. "You got my money?"

After beating Abel to a bloody pulp, Damon offered to let him work off his debt by turning his place into a crack house. Having already lost his soul, Abel figured that he didn't have much more to lose. He walked away into the night, leaving everything behind, except this raging dope habit that wailed like a banshee in the winter wind.

He called Bridgette who told Abel that Max had checked into rehab. She suggested that Abel do the same and offered him the number to a local recovery center. He hung up before she finished talking.

The next day the owners called and wanted to inspect the property. He stalled them for as long as he could, packed up what few clothes he had into a plastic trash bag and got Jay to drive him to the Greyhound station. He left behind his journals and other stuff he couldn't use.

Jay and Abel hustled up enough money to buy another rock before he left, but Abel felt tired and weary after the first hit, setting down the pipe and lowering his head to his hands. It was time for a rest. He headed back to Eden Valley as celestial sounds scintillated through his cocaine soaked brain.

Abel's parents agreed to take him in one last time. "No drugs. None of your old friends. No stealing," his father said.

"Things will be different this time," Abel promised.

He stopped by the gas station where Jay worked. Jay was just getting off work.

"Hey, gimme a minute to wash up and we'll go for a cruise, got time?"

"Nothing but," Abel said. An hour later, they were nodding in narcotic bliss. He needed to ease the pain of his life and he didn't care about the consequences. He just wanted to cover up the pain the only way he knew how.

Abel's parents went to a conference in Honolulu. While they were gone, he started dealing drugs out of the house. He began to drive to Los Tecatos three times a week to pick up a small quantity. Jay helped him to divide it into $20 and $50 bags. For a while, the money was flowing plentifully enough for him and Jay to keep their habits going.

One day a connection pulled a switch on him and he ended up with some bunk dope. The first gram was potent. He could barely keep his eyes open during the drive back to Eden Valley. The next morning he prepared his wake-up dose and shot up.

Abel waited for the dope to take effect. Nothing. Maybe he needed a little more. He put another quarter gram in the cooker, cooked it up and shot it. Nothing still. "Damn," he said. He had spent his last dollar on a bunch of worthless junk. He didn't even have enough money to drive back down to Los Tecatos to try getting his money back. Besides, some of those guys were hooked up with Los Vatos Locos. He didn't know if making a big stink would have been worth the trouble.

He was desperate. He searched the house until he found his parent's checkbook. He tore off a check from the back of the book. He took a canceled check from the files and copied the signature by laying the blank check on top of the canceled one, and held it up to the light. He wrote out the check for $120 and made it payable to himself. He knew he would eventually get found out, but he didn't want to think about that yet. He just wanted a fix. He was sick and he needed to do whatever he had to do to get well, even if it meant stealing from his parents again.

He drove into Los Tecatos and picked up enough dope to get him through the day. Then he called Jasmine. She invited him to spend the weekend with her in Reston Beach. He needed a change of pace. While he was there, he borrowed $100 from her and headed back to Los Tecatos. He picked up a gram of heroin and drove back up to Eden Valley to start dealing again.

Jay told him that he had several customers already lined up and promised that he'd help him double his money in a couple of hours.

"Meet me back here in three hours," Jay said as he handed him the last of the heroin. They had just shot up half of it themselves, and he figured he wouldn't be sick until later that night. By that time, he planned to have bought another two grams already.

He waited and waited. Jay never showed up. When he went by his house, his mother told him he had taken off in a hurry and said he was going out of town for the weekend. Burned.

Abel didn't have a choice. He had to come up with enough money to support his habit for another day. He grabbed the checkbook again. This time he wrote it for $300. He hated himself. He promised himself that he was going to put the money back before the day was over. He was going to sell part of his dope after saving enough to get loaded and put the money back.

Then his parents discovered that $420 was missing from their checking account. They knew that he had ripped them off again. That was it. They'd had enough.

They ordered him to pack up all of his stuff and never come back again. He loaded up his car and headed south on the Left Coast Highway.

Abel stopped in Los Tecatos and scored a $20 bag of heroin. He had a box of brand new insulin syringes in his trunk and traded a few of them for some more dope. "Hey, you wanna sell your car, man?" asked one of the dealers who congregated around the corner where he was buying dope.

"How much you give me for it?" he asked.

"I give you five grams, homes." That was equivalent to about $500.

"No thanks, man."

Abel ended up selling the car to a local used car dealer for $800. He bought five grams of heroin and rented a motel room.

Teresa was a dope dealer who had connections in Mexico, where she had come from illegally with her son Juan. Teresa had been selling dope in Los Tecatos for the last five years but had recently gotten so strung out that she was now broke and on the verge of eviction. He took Teresa to the motel with him where they shot dope, had wild sex in the Jacuzzi, and drank wine coolers.

"Promise that you'll never leave me, Abel," she sighed as she held him to her devil-tattooed breast.

The Jacuzzi brought him back to the womb and they nodded out together in narcotic ecstasy.

Teresa and Abel lived together with her son in her two-bedroom apartment. They sold dope, shot dope, smoked crack, had sex, and drank wine. Life was perfect.

He actually believed her when she told him that somebody had pulled a switch and given her a bag of coffee instead of a gram of heroin. No problem, he still had another $200.

One day as he was about to shoot up in the garage, Teresa came in and started yelling and swearing in Spanish. When she left, he noticed she had stolen his dope. That was it. He was out of there.

He made some phone calls and hooked up with Jay, who now lived and worked out of an old Dodge van, shoplifting and doing whatever other petty hustles he could. Jay offered Abel a dime of smack if he returned a pair of gloves to the department store where he had just stolen them.

"I hope you don't mind, but we're taking on a partner," Jay said.

"What for?" Abel asked, scratching his face, eyes half closed.

"You'll see," Jay replied as the van pulled into a motel parking lot. "Come on." Abel reluctantly followed Jay to a room at the rear of the motel.

Jay knocked on the door with a secret rhythm and the curtains ruffled as someone peeked outside. The door opened and a skinny, stringy haired girl with missing front teeth peeked out.

"Don't just stand there, hurry up and come in" she barked, her voice harsh and husky like a longtime whiskey drinker who smoked two packs of Camels a day. The woman motioned them inside and closed the door behind them. The room was dark and dingy and filled with smoke.

It wasn't until Abel's eyes adjusted to the dim light that he realized the woman in the room was Cindy Summers, the one who snitched him out to the cops for selling mescaline. "If it isn't the rat," he said. Abel looked at her in disgust and stepped toward her menacingly. Cindy covered her face and cowered toward the ground as Jay grabbed Abel by the arm.

"Cool it, man," Jay said. "That was a long time ago and she paid for what she did big time, didn't you Cindy?" Jay looked at Cindy.

Abel took a deep breath and stepped back.

"I'm so sorry, Abel," Cindy looked at the floor while she talked, almost in a whisper. "I was afraid they were going to lock me up and they told me if I bought some drugs on campus they would let me go." She looked up as tears slid down her pock marked face, her heavy makeup slimed down her cheeks like mud. "The cops weren't even after you. They wanted me to buy from Jay." She put her hand on Jay's arm. "But he wasn't around. Then I saw you and you asked me if I wanted to buy. They were watching me. I had to. I didn't want to, but I had to. I'm sorry. Please forgive me."

Abel lit a cigarette and handed the pack to Jay. Jay tapped out a smoke and offered it to Cindy. Abel grabbed the pack out of Cindy's hand and put it back in his pocket. He shook his head and looked back at Jay. "Why are we dealing with this snitch?"

"We all know what she did to you and that was wrong. But what you don't know is that the cops wanted her to keep on busting people, including me, Yogi, everybody. She felt so bad about what she did to you that she told the cops no. They reneged on their deal and sent her to Youth Authority and put her in general population. You know what they do to rats in there."

Abel took a drag of his cigarette and blew the smoke out slowly as he nodded. "Yes. I know what happens to them. I've seen it. Not pretty." He looked at Cindy and said, "You're lucky you made it out alive."

Cindy wiped her eyes with the back of her needle-scarred hand. "Yeah, real lucky. Hey, look at me, the lucky one! Ain't I special?" She laughed then started coughing with a deep hacking that sounded like she was going to blow a lung.

Abel cracked a hint of a smile and sat down in the chair. "So, what's the plan?"

Cindy joined Abel and Jay on a crime spree throughout Angel City. Boost and refund was a simple game. One of them would shoplift an item and the other one would return it to the store for a cash refund, saying it was a gift that they didn't want. Their hustle took them all over southern California, from as far north as Franklin Valley down to Red County, and as far to the east as Riverton. They averaged about three hundred dollars a day, but it all went to dope. They were shooting up over a gram of heroin a day apiece, and any money they had left over went to pay for gas, cigarettes, and an occasional box of donuts. At night, they'd shoot dope until they nodded out of existence, only to awaken to the startling fist of reality punching them in the gut every morning, shaking, sweating and doubled over from withdrawals. They always said they were going to save a wake up, but it never happened.

Sometimes Cindy would go out and turn a few tricks while Jay and Abel boosted and refunded. If they got enough money, they'd buy a quantity of dope to sell with hopes of getting their money back. Mostly they just got loaded, and kept on getting loaded until they were broke again.

Cindy was out selling herself. Abel and Jay were cruising into Red County looking for a new Larjey Department Store. They were both smacked back to the max and knew that it was time to hustle some more cash before the dope wore off. As they headed down the highway, their conversation drifted to the philosophical and religious. "God loves me," Abel said.

Jay snorted and shook his head. "How could God love a lowlife thief?" he asked.

"When Jesus was crucified, He told the thief on the cross beside him that he would join him in Paradise."

"What kind of God would let anybody hang him on a cross in the first place?" Jay laughed and scratched his head.

Abel was silent for a moment. He really wasn't sure why Jesus had died. "I don't understand it all. I just know that God loves me no matter what I've done or what I'm doing. He's watching me now, even as we speak."

"You're one crazy fool. This stuff got you talking crazy. If God loved you so much, why does He let you live like this?"

Again, Abel was silent. He slipped into a nod as he contemplated the nature of his relationship to the creator. "God help me," he whispered.

"God ain't nothing but another white man who don't give a damn about you, brother."

Abel thought about what he said for a moment as he nodded, eyes half-closed, and took a slow drag off his cigarette. "What if God was black?" he asked.

Jay began laughing uncontrollably.

It was late November, about a week before Thanksgiving, as they headed down Velvet Boulevard into Angel City. They were both nodding and scratching like the lost junkies that they were. Jay could barely keep his eyes open as he weaved through traffic like a snake, dodging cars by inches and flipping them off if they dared look at him funny.

Abel entered the Larjey and tried his best to look halfway like a real shopper. Something told him they were watching him. Maybe it was just his drug-induced paranoia, he told himself half-convincingly. He picked up a pair of slacks, laying them over his arm neatly. He turned and headed down another aisle, this time deftly slipping a belt and a handful of silk ties beneath the pants. He then headed to the dressing room to do his dirty work. He entered an empty stall and wrapped the belt and ties around his waist, covering them with his shirt. He tucked the shirt in carefully and straightened out his jacket, making sure nothing was bulging or hanging out. Then he exited the dressing room and put the pants back on the rack where he had found them.

They're watching you. Eyes piercing your soul. You're naked for everybody to see. Don't you know that everyone is watching you now? You can't hide anymore. They all know. They all see you. They hear your thoughts. The sound of your pounding heart echoes over the loud speakers as all of the store personnel and all of the customers stop and listen. They turn toward you and watch you with accusing eyes. Penetrating eyes burn with laser intensity through your naked soul. No place to run. No place to hide. It's over now. They know what you've done. They know who you really are. They all see you. You're naked.

Abel was in a movie watching himself play out that final scene. But he couldn't change the script, trapped in this moment of destiny. He watched from the audience as two security guards tackled him just outside the front door. Like a video recorder, the action stopped and then replayed itself in slow motion. He watched as they cuffed his hands behind his back and dragged him into the security office. He saw the police officers come in, place him under arrest, and haul him down to the station.

CHAPTER 21

THE AWAKENING

*

A star ignites
As angel's flight
breaks moon swept sky.
Between the darkness of the lonely night
and morning light.

A wounded warrior,
lost from home,
weary with the weight of wicked days gone by,
stirs suddenly from slumbered bliss,
moved by stillness,
awakened by the silent sounds
of dreaming.

The light of Grace appears
beside his sleeping form,
kissing him
with gentle lips
delicate against his ragged face.

Her healing wings
embrace him.
Tender hands
retrace his pain filled past
as scars dissolve
like fears without a trace.

He lifts his eyes toward the light
of mystic night and sees her face
shining like the sun
from heaven's place
and knows that he is home
again at last.

The police booked Abel into the Angel County Jail and charged with multiple counts of petty theft, possession of narcotics paraphernalia, fraud, and conspiracy.

The jail was a horrible place to kick a heroin habit. He was sick to his soul. Every cell in his body screamed in pain as he sat in one crowded holding cell after another.

In one cell, a couple of black guys were arguing about the Bible. One of them said, "You ain't got nothing but jail house religion."

The other man responded, "Jesus is real and the Bible is true. I've been set free."

"Free?" You ain't free, brother. You locked up in here with the rest of us losers." He looked around the cell and laughed mockingly. "Talking 'bout he free. Ain't this a trip?"

"Whom the Son sets free is free indeed."

Abel let their argument fade into the background as he doubled over in pain. He crawled over to the toilet and began heaving his guts until nothing but yellow bile trickled from his lips. Then dry heaves, shudders and shivers. Even his hair seemed to hurt. He looked at himself in the mirror. He looked old and tired. His eyes were faded with weariness. The tears flowed down his cheeks and his nose ran uncontrollably.

Sick with agonizing withdrawal symptoms, he stood meekly before the judge as he read the charges before the court. "I understand that you choose to waive your right to representation. Is that correct?"

"Yes, your honor."

"You also have the right to a speedy trial. Do you hereby waive that right?"

"I do."

"How then do you plead to the charges brought before this court?" he asked.

"Guilty," he uttered, head down in shame.

"Is there anything you'd like to say on your own behalf before I pronounce sentencing?"

"I hate myself."

BANG! BANG! BANG! The judge slammed his gavel. "The court hereby sentences you to eighteen months in the County Jail. Bailiff, return the defendant to custody."

Abel began to cough and gag until he doubled over in pain on the courtroom floor as the bailiff dragged him back into the holding cell.

He kept getting sicker and sicker. Usually withdrawal symptoms begin to subside within three to five days. He had been in jail for over a week now and he was still getting sicker. He could barely get out of bed. His appetite was gone. He couldn't catch his breath, and his side ached as if pierced by a sword. His soul ached with despair and utter self-contempt. Loneliness embraced him. He prayed for death. He saw a pocket-sized New Testament on the floor beside his bunk. He picked it up and put it in his jumpsuit pocket.

He called his mom. She told him she didn't want anything more to do with him. He was on his own. Three days later, Grace came to visit him. It was Thanksgiving.

They sat facing each other through a glass partition and talked through a telephone. "I saw your mother at church last Sunday and she told me you were here," she said.

"I'm glad you came," Abel replied.

"Why are your eyes so yellow? You need to see a doctor."

"They don't care about junkies here. They get hundreds of guys like me coming in here every day, kicking all kinds of dope. I'm just a number."

"Maybe this is what you get for all your sins. Maybe this is what you got coming." She shook her head slowly, sadly.

He hung up the phone, stood up and turned away.

The next thing he remembered was looking up at the ceiling. A white light glared down at him. The room was white. A man in white looked down at him and laughed. The man put his face close to Abel's and stared into his eyes mockingly. He turned to his assistant and said, "Hey, you want to see what a black guy with jaundice looks like?" Abel couldn't see who he was talking to at first, but he knew that someone else was in the room. Abel whispered, "What's going to happen?"

"Looks like you'll probably be dead by Christmas," the man in white jeered. His laughter faded into the sterile walls as the words echoed in his brain, "...DEAD BY CHRISTMAS"... "DEAD BY CHRISTMAS"...."DEAD BY CHRISTMAS." This was Thanksgiving Day. He closed his eyes as he slipped in and out of consciousness.

He saw her – first as through a glass darkly. Then face to face. He felt as though he knew her even as he was known. Gentle features, amber eyes, and a smile as delicate as rose petals dancing in the breeze. She looked down upon him and melted his heart with the warmth of her compassion. A single tear slid down her cheek and fell upon his lips. "Who are you?" The question escaped his lips with a whisper.

"Grace." Then she vanished into the nothingness from whence she came.

You're going to die and it matters to no one, least of all to you. At last, the pain of this life will end and you will cease to destroy the lives of all whose paths you've crossed. You think back over the years of running through people's lives like a hurricane, leaving behind only broken glass and splinters. There is nobody left to turn to. The world will be a better place without you as your life now comes to its vile and well-deserved finality: to die in jail, alone.

The Three Assassins stand by your bedside. Fear, Guilt and Resentment taunt you with every sin you have ever committed. They shout their filthy curses and accusations at you until you cover your ears with your hands and beg them to stop. And they don't stop. You know you have to end it all. You are beyond hope, beyond salvation. The Light is gone!

Abel wrapped the bed sheet around his neck and tied it into a hangman's noose, tying the end to the top of the bars. He leaped into the Abyss.

Then pain. The scarlet thread wrapped itself around his neck like an umbilical cord. He was drowning in an amniotic sea of Primordial Death. Panic poured out like water; his bones were out of joint. The cords of death entangled him; the torrents of destruction overwhelmed him. The cords of the grave coiled around him; the snares of death confronted him.

The Three Assassins stalked him. Surrounded him. Like roaring lions tearing their prey, they opened their mouths wide against him, engulfing him. He was lost in the Abyss. *My God, my God. Why have you forsaken me?*

Suddenly he awakened, sweating, screaming, and gasping for breath. The sheets twisted around his neck as the nightmare faded into the nothingness. Had he been asleep, dreaming that he was awake? Or was he still dreaming?

As he laid there in his bunk, he reached for the little Bible that was in his pocket. He flipped through its pages casually for a moment as he recalled the times he had used its pages for rolling tobacco, and thrown the book across the room in disgust. His eyes fell upon the words, *I am the Light of the world.*

He flipped the pages to beginning of the Book of John. As he began reading, a light seemed to ignite inside his head, like a bolt of lightning from east to west across the night. It all began to make such perfect sense. This Jesus that he was reading about was actually a real person who had said and done the things described in this book. The illumination began to spread from his head to his heart as he continued reading. He experienced the reality of Christ, the crucifixion and the resurrection. He remembered his baptism and knew that this was just symbolic of the deeper reality of being buried with Christ and raised again with Him, and that God had always been with him even from the foundations of the world. As he concluded the Book of John, the Light embraced him, and he knew that he had never been alone, and that he was a child of the Light throughout eternity.

Waves of light cascaded over him and he let go of all the hatred and rebellion that had filled his heart since birth. Fear, Guilt, and Resentment, the Three Assassins that had been his constant tormentors, were forced to flee by the power of the Light. The Light was within him and all around him.

He stood before the mirror again. The yellow tinge in his eyes had cleared beneath the tears. He took a deep breath, whispered thanks to God, and knew that he was free.

***

Further tests confirmed the jaundice was clear and Abel was completely healthy, as though he had never been sick at all. The doctor released Abel from medical isolation, shaking his head in astonishment.

Abel returned to his cell and sat for many days in silent stillness as he was so led by the Light and taught all things. He wrote his story on yellow legal tablets as it came to him in divine remembrance. In doing so, he remembered the 12 steps of recovery, this time knowing his higher power in a powerful, personal way as the Light within. He slowly began sharing his story with other prisoners, one by one, and encouraged them to seek the Light.

The Light gave Abel the gift of forgiveness and the ability to forgive others. The Light gave him the ability to love those who had hurt him. These two gifts – forgiveness and love – were his salvation, his grace.

The by-product of his new ability to forgive and love was an overwhelming sense of peace. This was much different from the mystical and drug-induced experiences of peace that he had known before. The old tranquility had been more of a detachment, a resignation, a narcotic anesthesia. It had seemed real enough in its day, but now he could see how empty it was. What he had been seeking so desperately for so long outside of him in every direction was that Light which was closer than his own breath all along. The first step to peace was to stand still in the Light.

CHAPTER 22

HOME AGAIN

*

Eyes stared back, with lies,
Through misty haze,
As smiles, dissolved by hate, retrace
Behind the wicked winter's fierce embrace.

We finally met again
As Springtime's sunlit shadows laced
Our eyes met once again.
This time in grace,
With light from ancient distant dawning days.

We glanced away
In shyness of a final fond embrace
Then turned toward each other once
Again as if to gaze
With longing and remembering,
Into Heaven, face to face.

Abel stood outside Angel County Jail on a February midnight beneath an auspicious new moon. He stepped out into the city streets and stood beneath a starlit night, a bright red neon sign above the city skyscrapers flashed the words JESUS SAVES against the grey buildings. He prayed for guidance as he stood in front of the concrete mausoleum that had been his home for the past thirteen months. He carried an accordion file containing pages of yellow legal tablets on which he had written his thoughts and a chronicle of his experiences. He knew that he was not alone.

Abel heard a horn honking in the distance and then the husky purr of the engine. He lifted up his eyes, lights shining toward him from the long darkness. A silver Jaguar appeared before him with Grace behind the wheel. She pulled up next to him, "Are you ready to come home?"

Abel stood in wonder as she stopped the car and got out. They embraced. "I'm so glad you came," he said. "I can't believe you're here."

"Believe it," Grace replied. She pulled away from the curb and headed back toward Eden Valley. Along the way Grace told Abel what had happened to the people they were close to. "I have some really bad news to tell you," she began "It's about my brother, Jay." Her eyes began to glisten.

"What happened?"

"Well you probably remember that Jay was hanging out with Cindy Summer."

"Yeah, I was with them before I got busted."

"I know. Jay really loved you like a brother," she continued, her voice trembling. "He's dead now! Dead!" Grace pulled to the side of the road and put her head down on the steering wheel, weeping uncontrollably.

Abel put his arm around her. "I'm so sorry, he murmured."

They sat beneath the starlit night, silent and still, except for the sound of Grace's soft sobs.

"Let's go someplace where we can talk," Grace said. "Do you mind driving?"

They pulled into a Denny's restaurant and ordered coffee. Grace composed herself and continued the tale. "I wanted to tell you last week when I came to visit you, but I didn't want to talk about it then. It's been so crazy in Eden Valley. Since you've been gone, it's like everything has been falling apart."

Abel reached across the table and held her hand. She looked at him and smiled.

"Do you want to talk about it now?" Abel asked.

Grace nodded and took a deep breath. She picked up a napkin and wiped her eyes. "Jay and Cindy started pulling armed robberies all across the state. They got greedy. They couldn't stop. They got in a shootout with the police and they died in a hail of gunshots like Bonnie and Clyde. It was all over the evening news."

"Grace." Abel held her hands tightly. "I don't know what to say."

"You don't have to say anything. It happened and nobody can change it."

"When did it happen?"

"Almost a year ago. Not long after you went away."

The waitress brought their coffee. "Anything else?" she asked.

Abel shook his head. "No thanks."

He added cream and sugar to his coffee and passed them to Grace. "Sorry, I should have asked you first. Cream and sugar?

"No thanks. I like it black, just the way I like my men." She laughed.

Abel laughed with her and shook his head "I cannot believe you said that. I thought you were Miss Goody Two Shoes."

"I still am. I can't believe I said it either."

They both laughed uncontrollably, falling down in their seats, and the other customers stared at them.

Grace took a slow sip of her coffee. "Without God I couldn't have gone through all this. I just wish Jay had turned his life around before he died. I tried so hard to get him to go to church." She hung her head.

Abel touched her chin. "I'm just glad that I accepted God's grace before it was too late."

Grace looked up and smiled. "You mean...?"

"Yes. I knew I was on my way to certain death. I finally saw the Light."

Grace clapped her hands in glee. "Oh, Abel. Thank God. I'm so happy for you. You just don't know how many times I prayed for you. I thought about you so much. I missed you so, so much." She got up and came around to Abel's side of the table, sliding in next to him in the booth. She leaned her head against his shoulder. "I'm so glad you're ok."

"Me too. I'm just glad that I found the Light before it was too late."

"You're one of the fortunate ones. It wasn't just Jay and Cindy that didn't make it."

"What do you mean?"

"You heard what those guys did to Yogi while he was prison?"

"Yeah, that was messed up. He didn't deserve that."

"He died in prison from complications related to AIDS."

"Aw, man." Abel shook his head in disbelief. "AIDS?"

"You know I'm a nurse now?"

Abel nodded. "I heard. That's great."

"That's how I found out. I work at different hospitals in jails and prisons."

He sighed and shook his head. "I still can't believe these guys are gone – Jay, Cindy, Yogi, who else?

"You remember Lola?"

"Yeah, I used to go out with her," Abel said. "That was a long time ago," he added.

"I'm sorry to be the one to tell you but Lola moved to Angel City and worked as high priced call girl. She was killed by one of her Johns."

"Anything good happen while I was gone?"

"Your mom and dad are doing well."

"As usual."

"They wanted me to tell you that they still love you and want you to do well."

Abel motioned to the waitress. "Can you bring us some water, please?" He looked to Grace. "You want water?"

"Please."

"I'll be right back," the waitress said.

Abel and Grace sat silently for a moment as the waitress set two glasses of water on the table.

"Oh, I almost forgot to tell you. Hillary Raincross has her own talk show now."

"What? Last thing I remember was when her parents sent her to a rehab center."

Grace laughed. She left after about a year or so, and then went to journalism school. She married some big television producer and now she has her own talk show."

"That's amazing. What does her father think?"

"The judge? He's proud of her."

Speaking of Judge Raincross, I've got some amends to make.

They headed back to the car. "Do you mind driving?" Grace handed Abel the keys.

Abel turned the key and the Jaguar purred to life. He turned to Grace and said, "I don't think I'm ready to go back to Eden Valley right now."

They pulled up in front of Genesis Manor. It was two o'clock in the morning and only a small light in the office remained lit. Abel knocked lightly not wanting to wake up the residents. Grace stood by his side. The door opened slowly and Billy Rydell stood there scratching his head. "What the...?" He opened his arms wide and gave Abel a big bear hug. "Well, look what the cat dragged in."

"I need your help," Abel said.

Billy opened the door wide and motioned for Abel and Grace to come in.

"This is my friend Grace," Abel told him. Billy reached out and shook her hand.

Billy led them to the office and poured coffee. "I'm usually not here this time of night. I'm the executive director now, but my night shift counselor went out and got drunk last night, so here I am. It must have been a God thing, because I am so glad to see you again, Abel."

"I'm glad to see you, too, Billy. It's been a long time. By the way, I want to start by saying I'm sorry for how I ended things here. I abused my position as phone counselor and I'm willing to do whatever it takes to make up for any harm that I caused to the program."

"Do I detect the sound of step nine?" Billy asked, cupping his hand to his ear.

"Made direct amends to people we had harmed, except when to do so would injure them or others," Abel said.

"Right on, Abel. So how long do you have clean and sober now?"

"Thirteen months," Abel replied. "But it was all in lockup. In fact, I just got out tonight."

"Thirteen months is thirteen months and if you can stay clean and sober in jail, you can do it anywhere. If it's anything like how it was the last time I was down, there's more dope on the inside than there is anyplace else."

"True," Abel said. "I still need to work on step nine though. I hurt a lot of people and I need to make it right."

"Well, I can tell you how you can make amends to Genesis Manor. You can come to work here. I need another night counselor."

"When do you want me to start?"

"You can start tonight."

Abel walked Grace to the car. "I've got a job," he said as he wrapped his arms around her.

Grace kissed Abel on the lips. "I love you Abel Adams."

Abel said, "I've always loved you Grace."

They stood silently beneath the stars.

***

Golden rays of healing light
In the name of Jesus Christ

Amen.
I am
Set free.

Angels stand before the night
Protecting me from hidden flight
Amen.
I am
At peace.

Peace abides my heart tonight
Faith affords my soul delight
Amen.
I am
With thee.

Far beyond this earthly light
Perfect dwelling place in sight
Amen.
I am
Thy seed.

Abel stood at the bottom of the long driveway. He stood and closed his eyes for a moment in the silent stillness of the Light before he began what seemed like a mile long walk toward his parent's house. His father was sitting on the front porch reading the latest edition of Scientific American. Abel stopped for a moment as he saw his father and thought about all the harm that he had caused his family. His father saw him, ran toward him, fell on his neck, and kissed him.

Abel said to him, "Father, I've done so much wrong in my life that I'm not worthy to be called your son."

His mother opened the door. She stood and wept as he put his arms around her. "Come in," she said.

***

Abel rang the doorbell to the grand estate. Judge Raincross came to the door, wearing a red silk smoking jacket, a large Dublin pipe in his hand. The judge took a puff of the cherry tobacco as he eyed Abel suspiciously. "What are you doing here?"

"I want to tell you I'm sorry for what I did," Abel said.

Judge Raincross closed the door behind him and stepped onto the porch. "You've done your time. You don't need to apologize to me."

"I stole your Christmas presents." Abel looked the judge in the eye, making sure the implications of what he was saying were fully understood.

"You did what?" The judge dropped his pipe on the concrete porch and his face turned red. He balled his fists at his sides, breathing heavily.

"I was the one who broke into your home about ten years ago and stole your family's Christmas presents." Abel hung his head in shame. "I did a lot of wrong to a lot of people and while I was in jail, I had a spiritual awakening. I saw the Light and now I want to make up for the wrongs I did to all the people I've hurt. I've been clean and sober for over a year now and I'm working as a substance abuse counselor. I'm here to make amends."

Judge Raincross stared at Abel for a moment and his features softened. He bent over to pick up his pipe, tapping it against his palm. "Come in." He opened the door and motioned Abel to follow him inside the house.

Mrs. Raincross came down the stairs. "Who was at the door, honey?" She stopped when she saw Abel standing in the foyer.

"You remember Mr. Adams," the judge said, pointing to Abel.

She smiled nervously, "Of course I do. Your father is a professor at the university, isn't he?"

"Yes, he is. I'm sorry for everything," Abel said.

The judge motioned for Abel to have a seat. "Have a seat while I speak to my wife in private for a moment." The judge and his wife stepped into the kitchen.

"He did what?" Mrs. Raincross shouted. Abel heard the sound of a glass falling and breaking on the floor.

Abel looked at the front door contemplating his escape. He imagined they were going to kill him and bury his body in the back yard. He prayed silently for serenity and courage. He tapped his fingers together nervously as the couple reentered the room. They sat down on the sofa across from him. The judge lit his pipe again.

"Mr. Adams," he began, "Our family was devastated that Christmas. We couldn't believe that anybody could be as cruel and callous as to steal the gifts right from under our tree." Mrs. Raincross pursed her lips and nodded in agreement.

"Although the insurance company made up for the financial losses, it took us a long time to get over the emotional losses. Somebody, you, violated the sanctity of our home, violated our sense of peace and safety. How does anyone ever get over something like that?"

Abel put his head down in his hands, weeping in shame and regret. "I know that just saying I'm sorry can never make up for I did to you and your family. I just want you to know that I will do whatever it takes to make it up to you." Abel looked up. "I don't know how you ever get over something like that."

"We realized that whoever stole from us had to be some lost soul," Mrs. Raincross began. "We prayed for him, whoever he was, this thief, this poor lost soul. We prayed that he would someday find the grace of God's love and peace."

The judge held his wife's hand. "Looks like our prayers were finally answered," he said.

Mrs. Raincross interjected. "You know, our daughter, Hillary, was running amuck, strung out on dope, hanging out with all kinds of lowlifes – no offense."

"None taken," Abel replied.

"Well, we didn't know what else to do, so we sent Hillary to a substance abuse treatment center. She went through a place called Genesis Manor in Cornerstone and finally got her act together. She's been on the straight and narrow ever since."

"Genesis Manor? I work there," Abel said.

A smile appeared on Judge and Mrs. Raincross' lips. The judge cleared his throat. "Must be a God thing," he said. "Hillary has been clean for over ten years now. She's married to a wonderful man and she has a great career. We're very proud of her."

"I'm glad to know she's doing well," Abel said. "I just want to make up for all the wrong I've done and hopefully help someone else to see the Light."

"We are people of faith and we've agreed to forgive you for what you did to us. There is one condition, though."

Abel looked up in shock took a deep breath. "I'll do anything."

"Just tell your story, Abel. Tell your story."

***

Abel sat on the set of The Hillary Show in front of the studio audience. He wore a blue sport jacket over a white shirt and khaki pants. Hillary Raincross sat on the couch next to him. She smiled at the audience and said, "Joining us today is my special guest and longtime friend, Mr. Abel Adams, who has an amazing story about his spiritual journey, recovery and enlightenment. You will not believe what this man has been through and how he came out on the other side. He's going to tell us a little bit about his story today. Let's all give Abel a big welcome."

Hillary led the audience in a round of polite applause.

Abel began, "Who am I? What is my purpose? What is my destiny? These are the fundamental questions. Love is the answer. Amo ergo sum. I love, therefore I am. Love is the source and destiny of being; the essence of life; the space between thoughts. Love is the Light; the Light is within us and all around us as the grace of God - so profound and so far reaching that it is almost impossible to imagine.

For many years I was asleep, dreaming that I was awake. Today, life continues as a series of miracles. Adversities became opportunities. Failures became successes. Darkness led me toward enlightenment. The awakening continues as destiny unfolds into the eternal. I am just beginning to see the Light and walk in it, moment by moment.

What I can tell you here is just a partial glimpse at what occurred in my life over the past quarter century. My journey began in the silent stillness of the Light where each of us can seek and find it right here and right now. Now is eternity. Thank you for letting me tell my story."

The audience stood up and applauded. Judge Raincross and his wife stood next to Grace in the front row. Abel's family was also in the front row, tears streaming down their faces. Aunt Delilah turned to Abel's mother and said, "I told you that boy was going to be a preacher."

After the resounding applause, Abel stood up and walked to the center of the stage. The audience sat down and Abel grabbed the microphone. He bent down on one knee, looked over to Grace, and said, "Lingering like a meandering fawn, through sycamore and oleander meadows, destiny dawns, as a cellar door opens unto a summer afternoon. Vermillion sun luminous across a sapphire sky. Harbors of memory sleep softly, surrendering in golden bliss to the passion of a lover's kiss. Lullaby hush, peaceful as a mother's smile. Cerulean melodies, lilting like laughing willows. Blue butterflies and golden sunflowers along a violet lake. Home again, at last. Tranquility, a moment in eternity. Fantastic grace, your lovely face, the sweet sound of you saying, 'Yes' to me asking, 'will you marry me?' Grace, will you please marry me?"

Grace ran up on stage, shouting, "Yes! Yes! Of course, I'll marry you, Abel Adams." They embraced on stage and the audience went wild.

Abel and Grace were married the following week. Abel's brother Jesse was his best man. His mother and father opened their home for the reception.

Nine months and a day later, Grace gave birth to their son. Abel stood in the delivery room by Grace's bedside. The doctor handed Abel the scissors and allowed him to cut the umbilical cord. As Abel cradled his little child in his arms, the baby's eyes slowly opened and what Abel saw was love personified. "I love you, my precious son," Abel whispered as a single tear traced its way gently down his cheek. For the first time, he knew tears of joy.

When we met
Glimpse of eternity
Broke through
A tesseract of time
Revealing
Names
Written next to one another
So close as almost touching
In the book
That was before
the worlds were formed
Beyond a certainty I knew it then
And even when
Time finds its end
There could never be
Another time as this
Such moment of destiny
As when we met.

EPILOGUE

✳

The day after finishing what I had hoped to be the final draft of this manuscript, Abel and I climbed to the top of a mountain overlooking Eden Valley. The sky was remarkably clear that morning, shaded by bold strokes of purple and gold, as we beheld the rising summer sun. Below, the incandescence of the city gently conceded to the radiance of dawn. The journey was far from over, however. The long walk up the down road, as Abel liked to refer to it, had just begun. "What's next?" I asked. Smiling, he slowly turned toward me and asked, "Have you seen the Light?"

I was afraid he was going to ask me that question one day, knowing that I would have to seriously contemplate its meaning. After hesitating for a moment, I gazed deeply into Abel's dark eyes and suddenly saw what seemed like ten thousand stars, scintillating and shimmering like diamonds against a velvet night. And in the center of all these stars was a silent stillness. The Light appeared within and all around him with such bright intensity that I had to look away close my eyes. And when I turned again toward him and opened my eyes Abel Adams was gone and all that remained was the Light.

A butterfly floated, fluttered and flew into the sun.

***

I sprinted all the way back down the mountain and headed toward home. The rising sun was still shining brightly on the horizon ahead of me nearly blinding me as I ran directly toward it. I shielded my eyes with my hand and kept running. Finally, I returned to my familiar apartment and slammed the door behind me. Almost out of breath, I sank down into the chair at my desk, powered up the laptop and blazed away on the keyboard. Suddenly, I stopped, sat and stared silently into space, surrendered, spent. I closed my eyes so nobody could see me. And I was gone.

REFLECTIONS IN THE LIGHT

✳

My depression deepened unbearably and finally it seemed to me as though I were at the very bottom of the pit. I still gagged badly at the notion of a Power greater than myself, but finally, just for the moment, the last vestige of my proud obstinacy was crushed. All at once I found myself crying out, "If there is a God, let Him show Himself! I am ready to do anything, anything!"

Suddenly, the room lit up with a great white light. I was caught up into an ecstasy which there are no words to describe. It seemed to me, in the mind's eye, that I was on a mountain and that a wind not of air but of spirit was blowing. And then it burst upon me that I was a free man. Slowly the ecstasy subsided. I lay on the bed, but now for a time I was in another world, a new world of consciousness. All about me and through me there was a wonderful feeling of

Presence, and I thought to myself, *So this is the God of the preachers!* A great peace stole over me and I thought, *'No matter how wrong things seem to be, they are still all right. Things are all right with God and His world.* ~Alcoholics Anonymous Comes of Age: A Brief History of A.A., p. 63

I saw that the grace of God, which brings salvation, had appeared to all men, and that the manifestation of the spirit of God was given to every man, with which to profit. These things I did not see by the help of man, nor by the letter, though they are written in the letter; but I saw them in the light of the Lord. I saw also that there was an ocean of darkness and death, but an infinite ocean of light and love, which flowed over the ocean of darkness. ~George Fox

And God said, Let there be light: and there was light. ~Genesis 1:3

The people walking in darkness have seen a great light; on those living in the land of the shadow of death a light has dawned. ~Isaiah 9:2

That was the true light that lights every man that comes into the world. ~John 1:9

I am the light of the world. Whoever follows me will never walk in darkness, but will have the light of life. ~John 8:12

Believe in the light that ye may be children of the light. ~John 12:36

God is light and in him is no darkness at all. ~1 John 1:5

There will be no more night. They will not need the light of a lamp or the light of the sun, for the Lord God will give them light. And they will reign forever and ever. ~Revelation 22:5

From within or from behind, a light shines through us upon things, and makes us aware that we are nothing, but the light is all. ~Ralph Waldo Emerson

The black moment is the moment when the real message of transformation is going to come. At the darkest moment comes the light. ~Joseph Campbell

In the right light, at the right time, everything is extraordinary. ~Aaron Rose

Someday perhaps the inner light will shine forth from us, and then we'll need no other light. ~Goethe

In faith there is enough light for those who want to believe and enough shadows to blind those who don't. ~Blaise Pascal

For light I go directly to the Source of light, not to any of the reflections. ~Peace Pilgrim

Who is more foolish, the child afraid of the dark or the man afraid of the light? ~Maurice Freehill

People are like stained-glass windows. They sparkle and shine when the sun is out, but when the darkness sets in their true beauty is revealed only if there is light from within. ~Elisabeth Kübler-Ross

I will love the light for it shows me the way. Yet I will endure the darkness for it shows me the stars. ~ Og Mandino

Your life is something opaque, not transparent, as long as you look at it in an ordinary human way. But if you hold it up against the light of God's goodness, it shines and turns transparent, radiant and bright. And then you ask yourself in amazement: Is this really my own life I see before me? ~Albert Schweitzer

The first step to peace is to stand still in the Light. ~George Fox

Robert Hammond

ABOUT THE AUTHOR

✳

ROBERT HAMMOND is an award-winning screenwriter, producer and bestselling author of over a dozen books, including Ready When You Are: Cecil B. DeMille's Ten Commandments for Success and Blockbuster Resumes: Insider Secrets for Dazzling Your Audience and Blowing Away the Competition. He earned an MFA in Creative Writing and is a highly sought-after speaker on personal achievement, creativity and recovery.

Hammond teaches screenwriting and develops literary properties for film and television. His film projects include the documentary One Day on Earth and epic adventure C.B. DeMille: The Man Who Invented Hollywood.

He is a former spokesperson for Capitol One Financial Corporation and has appeared on over 300 radio and television programs. His book, Life After Debt: Free Yourself from the Burdens of Money Worries – Once and for All sold over 100,000 copies.

Robert Hammond